SHAVE ICE

TOM STEVENS

THE MAUI PUBLISHING COMPANY • WAILUKU, MAUI, HAWAII

Library of Congress Cataloging-in-Publication Data
Stevens, Tom, 1946-
 Shave Ice
 1. Maui (Hawaii) — Social life and customs — Humor.
 I. Title.
DU628.M3S73 1989 996.9'21 89-3245
Library of Congress Catalogue Number 89-90985

ISBN 0-9622212-0-1 Softcover

Printed in the United States of America.

The watercolor painting by Wailuku artist Ann Uyehara that adorns the cover of this book uses two motifs familiar to islanders — shave ice and hanafuda cards. The popular Japanese "flower cards" usually decorated with plant designs are here shown with shave ice symbols — the ball of shaved ice itself, the flat wooden spoon, the straw, the conical paper cup and, of course, the colored syrup flavorings. In Uyehara's playful composition, these elements become parts of other island scenes, with each "card" tossed upon a tatami straw mat as in the hanafuda playing style. The artist's favorite shave ice flavor is "steady blue."

PREFACE

Hi. Thanks for picking up this book. The stories and photographs herein were first published between 1974 and 1988 by *The Maui News,* a kind and tolerant employer.

Many of the stories appeared in a Tuesday column called "Shave Ice," named for Hawaii's favorite summer confection. I had in mind something light, refreshing and colorful, and something that would appeal equally to islanders and newcomers.

I also wanted a title that would symbolize real island life rather than the glossy fabrications of the tourist media.

The Hawaiian Islands — and Maui in particular — have been so heavily developed, marketed and promoted since statehood that the images put forth in our media have become decidedly unreal. In the rush to create and sell "Paradise," Hawaii has been overlooked.

It has been my good fortune to work for one of the few publications which still views Hawaii as a real place; a place with a rich history and a strong, spirited, funny, life-loving populace. Most of the articles that follow could not have been published elsewhere in the state.

I thank *The Maui News* and its employees for putting up with me all these years — especially publishers J. Walter Cameron, Frances Cameron and Maizie Sanford; editor Nora Cooper; and my long-suffering newsroom bosses Earl Tanaka, Dave Hoff and Roy Tanaka.

Those who made this book possible include its instigator and editor, Nora Cooper, designer Cynthia Conrad of Faught & Miyashiro, cover artist and Maui girl Ann Uyehara, and production consultant Rich Van Scoy.

Kula photo sorceress Karen Porteus coaxed usable prints from my marginal exposures, and Kaui Goring took the flattering back jacket portrait. Thanks also to photographers Wayne Tanaka and Matt Thayer of *The Maui News* for their darkroom expertise.

For their long-time encouragement, I thank my dear friend Joan Frank of San Francisco and my beloved brother Mike, who led me on several of the adventures that follow.

I hope these stories and photos will bring you some of the laughter, insight and inspiration that Hawaii has shared with me.

Aloha,
Tom Stevens
Wailuku, 1989

TABLE OF CONTENTS

PEOPLE AND PLACES

WHIMSY

Moving the Things

Ooooh. The things are moving again!

They're so excited. The clothes are rocking in the closet, brushing up against each other and swinging on their hangers. The shoes clump time down below; big, knobby shoes, but happy, like peasants at a picnic. The belts slap the door like a fistful of eels.

Out in the room, objects stir and creak, straining to leave this place behind. Chairs, boxes, bookshelves; a bed, a lamp, a table. The rug flutters like a faint heart. Pictures rattle on the walls, and the records sing in their sleeves.

They were singing "Something in the way you move me" when I caught them the other day. That's their version of the Beatles hit. The things sing it every time we move now, so they're getting pretty good.

I stole up on them at lunch hour, having ducked out of work to do some quick packing. The things were singing with such gusto that they didn't hear me tiptoe down the hall.

"Something in the way you move me, moves me like no other mover ... Something in the way you place me ... don't wanna leave you now, don't wanna hear you howl ...."

"Shuddup!" I howled, banging the door open. I sprang into the room in a ninja crouch, as I had seen the samurai do in "Saga of the One-Armed Swordsman." I snapped my head around fiercely.

The wastebaskets, which had been dancing on the carpet, wheeled too slowly toward their places by the dresser. I ninja-kicked them into the wall. The coconut hats tittered.

"Who wants to move to the dump?!!" I roared. The hats fell silent. It was good to have their attention, but I could still hear the clothes conga-dancing in the closet behind me.

"Who wants to move to Ka Lima?!" I snarled, flinging open the closet door. "The next hanger squeak I hear — and it's off to the Alii Room!" That shut them up. I whirled to face an ugly brute of a chair that had given me trouble in the past.

"Who wants to move to Big G's?!" I challenged, squaring off. The chair is bigger, but I'm meaner — especially at moving time.

3

It rocked back into its corner. "Salvation Army?" I said next. The queen mattress sagged a little more, and the air around it filled with parachuting lice.

I stood panting in the center of the room. The things and I had reached our usual standoff — they happy because they were moving again, I bitter because I had to move them.

"None of you is indispensable, you know!" I raged. But even as I said it, I knew it was a scrofulous lie. The things smirked and traded glances. They knew the real score: I've been their prisoner for years.

As I contemplate my 37th lifetime move and 15th on Maui, I'm forced to admit that the things are still grimly in control. Many people feel that the trauma of moving is about leaving an old, comfortable place and going to a strange new one, but I disagree. The trauma comes from moving the things.

Where do they hide between moves? I mean, you have your little room set up — clothes folded here, pictures hung there, a few books on a shelf, a chair or two awaiting a visitor, a bed, a mirror. It looks like a monk's cell. Then you have to move, and a wall of boxes forms as high as the Pyrenees.

This prompts disdain from hip friends whose entire earthly possessions fit snugly under one eyelid. "Gahd, you have sooo much stuff!" they sniff. "Why don't you lighten up your life a little?"

Gahd knows I've tried — and I have gotten better over the years. When I was young and married, we had 1,200 records and a stereo system that could be heard on Mars. We had a "California King" bed, a punee, rattan armchairs, couches, a dining room set, a washer and dryer, a television, a piano, dishes that matched and croquet mallets that didn't. We needed a whole house just to put the things in.

Now older, wiser and much weaker, I own nothing I cannot carry with one arm. Furniture must be collapsible or inflatable, mats of lightest gauge lauhala, most books and records borrowed from the library. My stereo is so small I can put it under my shirt.

So where did all these other things come from? The three sets of elephant bookends, the bongo drums, the closet full of Alii Room clothes? And why do they follow me around?

I tell you, things have no sense at all.

— *July, 1988*

Pidgin

Wot?!

There is delicious irony in the state Board of Education's desire to ban pidgin speaking in public school classrooms because it is not the "standard English" supposedly used in business and higher education.

Wot iron-knee!? No talk sweef, you.

This corner feels that the Board of Education and the department it oversees have no right to call for standard English in the classroom, because they do not use standard English themselves.

'As right, dey mo worse.

Instead, the educators use a baffling, spineless, infuriating doublespeak I call "highfalutinese."

Geev um, brah. Step da neck.

What is highfalutinese? Let's use an example. In standard English, the traditional beginning reader sentence is: "See Spot run," or, in pidgin, "Chylook Spot."

The same sentence translated into highfalutinese would be: "The integrated ambulatory motor systems by intentional exercise of which the canine quadruped hereinafter identified as Spot facilitates self-propulsion at a medium- to high-velocity gait along a trajectory roughly contiguous with but not absolutely identical to the terrestrial surface is observed."

Broke da brain, garanz.

As the example illustrates, highfalutinese can be a severe handicap to its speakers, restricting them to dead-end jobs in the DOE and limiting their social circle to lawyers and Einstein.

Compared to highfalutinese, pidgin is a spunky, supple language, lively as a naughty hula, sly as a mongoose, that darts and weaves like a halfback in the barefoot league. It's also a wonderfully humorous language, a tongue with cheek.

Frankly, I don't see why this thing has to be either-or. Let's be bilingual. Teach standard English in the public schools and pidgin to everybody else.

I'd like to see a pidgin English course designed by the DOE. It wouldn't be called pidgin, of course — probably "Vernacular

Expression of Mid-Pacific Archipelagic Peoples, 201." It could be taught at night school, and the public school kids who learn standard English by day could moonlight as tutors.

The pidgin classes would be open to new residents, Canadians, vacationing soap-opera stars, windsurfers, Realtors and other pidgin-deprived people whose activities bring them into occasional contact with actual islanders:

"Howzit ladies and genamen, an you Realtahs, too — nah, nah, nah! E komo mai, you folts, an' welcome to da pidgin shkool. Wot I like know bot, if dis da shkool, an' I da teachah, den who da pidgins stay? Nah nah nah! OK, all serious aside, da firs ting chak erybody get da course silly-bos. Get? OK, chylook um. Like da firs page tell, today lesson stay 'jun ken po.' You live Hawaii, you gotta know dis: rock broke seezaz, seezaz cot papah, papah wrap rock."

In addition, a mobile pidgin "language lab" with an embarrassing, DOE-type name could visit luxury resorts, condo areas and other pidgin deprived neighborhoods. Headphone equipped "learning stations" inside the van would provide taped instruction, starting with simple everyday phrases:

"Good evening, and welcome to the Holo Holo Da Kine Talk-Mobile Living Language Lab. In this first lesson, we will conjugate the verb 'come stay go' and the basic greeting forms 'How you stay?', 'How you stay been?' and 'How you been stay been?' Popular retorts like 'No ack!' and 'Boddah you?' also will be covered, as will the universal filler expression 'da whachucall.'

"We'll start with an everyday situation. You are hungry. In standard resort English you might say: 'Darling, would you please have the butler call room service for cracked crab and caviar, and a bottle of Chateauneuf-du-Pape '57? You're such a dear.'

"Here is the same request in pidgin. Repeat each phrase slowly: 'Eh, I li' eat . . . Howzabout ast da whachucall, bottlah . . . call da kine . . . fo' send op tripe stew plate . . . side ordah fries mustahd-ketchup . . . nishime, tako poki, small bottle bagoong, rock salt, 10 California roll, pint Crown Royal. Tanks, eh?' "

If we were all bilingual, we'd realize that it's not how we speak that counts, but what we order.

— October, 1987

Mosquito Wars

Eeeeeeeen . . . eeeeeeeEEEEeeeeen . . . eeeeeeeeEEEEEEEE-
EEEEE!

Whap!

They always find the ear. And the forehead, and the foot that
crept out of the bedding. But they really go for the ear. I think
they like to see us slap our own heads in the middle of the night.
It makes their bloodsucking little lives worthwhile.

We're talking mosquitoes here, but we're also talking war. War
between huge, lumbering, sleep-drugged hominids and these
dancing kamikazes of the night, some no bigger than a flying
eyelash.

On our side we have Raid and mosquito coils — both nearly as
harmful to us as to the enemy. We have large spatulate hands
that can be smacked together, and apposable thumbs for snatching and grasping at the whining air. And we have screens.

On their side, they have the lightness of a bubble and the street
savvy that comes from hundreds of millions of years on the planet.
They're not fast, but they are superb aviators, maneuvering aloft
on handclaps of air, peeling off in formation for low-level strafing
runs, then barrel-rolling away again.

To them, we probably don't even seem to be sentient beings —
just vast, gently rolling foothills of flesh. The acreage of our faces
alone could accommodate a hundred of them, and sometimes does.
To us, they seem . . . invisible.

They are so tiny and light that they can touch down on our most
sensitive runways — eyelids, cheeks, the middle ear — and
engorge themselves before our distant early warning systems can
flash red alert.

They are also surprisingly resilient, as anyone will attest after
snatching one of these parasitic hang-gliders out of the air. Got
you, little devil! You grind the prey in your fist, then open your
hand expecting to see the oily gray smear that signals a kill. The
mosquito waits one beat to lull you off guard, then —
EEEEEEEEeeeeeeeeee — ascends in glory to fight another day.

Furious, you wheel around to renew the battle, sight in on the

7

target, raise your mighty arms . . . and the mosquito disappears. Poof. Vanishing as utterly as if it had entered another dimension. Leaving us dumbfounded — hulking, pitiful King Kongs driven to madness by a superior technology.

Mosquitoes. Did a just and loving God create them? Did the God who made the lamb make thee? I'm afraid so, though it's more comforting somehow to ascribe satanic origins to these purveyors of malaria, yellow fever and head-slapping midnights.

No, God made mosquitoes to keep us humble, to remind us of the greater order of things. We humans have been to the bottom of the ocean and to the icy summit of Mt. Everest. We have walked on the moon and invented deviled ham. But can we catch two mosquitoes in a row?

How do they get in? The screens are intact, and you didn't leave the door open. There are no stagnant ponds on the windowsills, no mulch of rotting leaves on the carpet. But they do find a way.

I got 12 mosquitoes one night, though. That was a great night, one small step for mankind. But the next night I realized I had won the battle and lost the war. They were back. Well, their relatives were back, anyway — and they attacked with the vengeance that can only follow the loss of loved ones.

I finally had to use the Raid. Ssssttt! Ssssttt! Die, sucking needlefaces!

The next morning, my own face looked like Ulumalu Road or the bottom of a jogging shoe. If I could have read braille, the bumps would have spelled: "Caution — something terrible has happened here."

Think of the patio parties that have to move indoors, the beach picnics that break up apologetically, the candlelight dinner on the lanai that doesn't get past the soup course. And think of all the tender tropic moments, pregnant with moonlight and romantic possibility, blitzed forever by a whining cloud of wrath.

Oh, they know what they do to us. They love it. I can almost hear their deedily, piping little voices as they mass for the assault:

"Wing commander to attack squadron leaders. Softball picnic overflight reports sleeping baby's face and arms uncovered; plump, succulent opu's hanging below T-shirt hems; pair of sweethearts embracing behind banyan tree. Do you read me? Over."

"Read you fivers, wing commander. All units aloft and armed, over."

"Attack squadron Anopheles, drain the baby. Squadron Culex, buzz softball player faces while squadron Aedes sweeps in on opu's from below. Drink deeply and take no prisoners. Over."

"Roger, wing commander. But what about the sweethearts? Over."

"Hyeh-heh-heh. I'll attend to them myself. Over and out." EEEEeeeeeeee.

They say there's a silver lining to every cloud, even a cloud of mosquitoes. Why, without them, we wouldn't have invented long sleeves, mesh netting and Cutter's lotion, though I'm not sure how pivotal these things are in the evolutionary march of our own species.

Our eye-hand coordination, albeit primitive when matched against the cunning aerobatics of our tormenters, would not have developed even this far. Without mosquitoes to keep our reflexes sharp, we would probably drop the toothpaste cap a lot more often and slap ice cream cones into our foreheads.

Yes, I suppose we should be grateful to mosquitoes in some twisted way. They have shaped our civilization, midwifed the evolution of our central nervous systems. You can thank them if you want. Not me. I don't like them at all.

On second thought, I am grateful for one thing. Have you ever seen a real close-up, electron microscope photo of a mosquito? Huge, killer eyes, robot legs scaled with vicious-looking spikes, a bladed metallic face that only a potato combine could love? We're talking "alien" here, alien to da max.

When I see those photos, I forget the itching bumps and ringing ears, the nights spent tracking mosquitoes into high corners and the depths of the closet, swatting, swiping, cursing, climbing onto furniture, knocking the philodendron over again.

Instead, I kneel down and thank God. Not for creating mosquitoes . . . but for making them smaller than us.

—November, 1983

Bears

For an island boy, this was to be the Backpacking Adventure of a Lifetime: a four-day trek through the storied "Grand Canyon of the Tuolumne," a remote section of California's Yosemite National Park famous for its sheer granite gorges, thundering waterfalls and dense evergreen forests.

"You'll love it," my brother Mike promised as we slung our packs onto our shoulders and crunched across the gravel toward the trailhead. "Hardly anyone ever goes here, so the river's choked with trout this time of year. They're so big their splashes will wake us at night. We'll need a gaff to land 'em."

"Gee," I marveled. As a lifetime island resident, I had never seen a trout, let alone "landed" one. I had also never seen a bear.

"Bears?" I asked, my voice quavering slightly. "Will there be bears?"

"Nah," my brother said with the hearty assurance of the weekend woodsman. "They'll all be farther south in the park, scrounging for garbage around the camps. Even if we do see one, all you have to do is bang a couple of tin cups together and yell at him, and he'll hightail it out of there. Bears are chicken."

"That's good," I said. "I wouldn't know what to do if I saw a bear."

"Just leave it to me, Timmy Bozo," he said. "I know how to handle bears."

The first part of the hike was magnificent — a 3,000-foot descent through pine forests and across granite domes into the Grand Canyon of the Tuolumne River. The trail was good, the air crisp, the river clear and icy. We saw no other hikers, but the significance of that escaped me at the time.

We started off singing "Fol-de-ri, Fol-de-ra!" and other woodsy songs from seventh grade music class, but by the time we staggered to a halt 10 miles later, all I could manage were gasps and wheezes. Hiking through Haleakala was never like this.

We camped by a deep, still pool at a bend in the river. My brother assembled his fly rod, humming to himself. I stumbled through the thick grass looking for a nice place to fall down and die.

"Get the burner started and oil the skillet," he ordered cheerfully. "We'll be eating monster trout in 15 minutes. This pool should be stuffed with them."

It was, too. There must have been hundreds of them — each the size of a jumbo paper clip. A sardine would have been Moby Dick in that pool. Finally, well after dark, Mike splashed back to camp and proudly displayed his catch.

"Look, a trout!" he said, holding by the tail a slender, spotted fish about five inches long.

"Good thing we brought the gaff," I smirked, stirring the vegetable-cheese-noodle goulash which would pass for that night's dinner.

Fortunately, we had packed in more than enough food for four days. Nothing light, of course, because Mike insists on fresh fruit and vegetables, cheese, wine, tinned goods, eggs, meat, rice, granola, loaves of bread, cookies and pancake mix while hiking. No panty, freeze-dried "trail food" for us.

One thing I'll say for those trail foods, though — they don't give off much scent in their sealed aluminum packets.

We got through the first night splendidly — those Lilliputian trout couldn't have splashed us awake if their lives depended on it. After a fashionably late breakfast of eggs Florentine and blueberry pancakes, we broke camp and set off along the river again, covering eight tough but scenic miles before sunset. As the light faded, we found ourselves in a vast, dark, spooky forest straight out of "Hansel and Gretel."

"I'm wasted," my brother said, slinging his pack down in a little clearing in the trees. "Let's camp here tonight — this looks like a good spot."

Good spot for a werewolf convention, I thought, but I was too tired to say so. We rolled out our sleeping bags, fired up the burner and prepared a savory dinner of tuna-cheese-vegetable goulash, Keoki coffee and oatmeal cookies. Aroma-wise, we could not have broadcast our presence more effectively with limburger.

After cleaning up, I crammed all of our remaining food into a nylon "stuff sack," tied it to a rope, threw the rope over a nearby branch and hoisted the bulging bag of goodies 15 feet into the air. I tied the free end of the rope to another tree, as high as I could reach.

"You still worried about bears?" Mike said, eyeing my flimsy attempt to bear-proof our food supply. "That won't even slow 'em down."

"It will, too," I replied. "It said so in my trail guide."

"Forget it," he laughed. "Besides, there aren't any bears around here ... see?" He swung his flashlight in an arc around our campsite, then walked a few paces into the woods, cupped his hands over his mouth and started bellowing into the darkness.

"Calling all bears!" he shouted. "Are you out there? Come and get it! Nice fresh food bag, hanging in the air!"

"Are you crazy?!" I said. "Now they'll know we're here."

"Relax," Mike chuckled. "Here, take these tin cups to bed with you, and if you see a bear, clink them together like I told you." With that, he rolled up in his sleeping bag and flicked off the flashlight . . . plunging us into utter, coal black, Stygian, primordial, "In the Beginning" darkness. "Nighty-night," he said.

"Do bears eat human flesh?" I asked.

"Nighty-night," he repeated, and started snoring.

I must have dozed off at some point, because I remember waking up. It wasn't that "bolt upright" kind of thing that follows nightmares or phone calls. It was much more insidious: strange noises in the night, hairs doing a little fear polka all over your body, and the dawning realization that You Are Not Alone.

I heard the noises first. Low, snuffling sounds and coughing grunts. The noises weren't loud, but they were very, very close . . . and they seemed to be coming from something very, very big.

"Now I lay me down to sleep," I whispered. "I pray the Lord my soul to keep. If I should die before I wake, I pray the Lord my soul to take Amen." I shivered in my sleeping bag, waiting for the stink of hot breath, the crunch of fangs, the decapitating slash of foot-long claws.

Nothing happened. The snuffling and grunting continued, and eventually I became curious. If I was going to die, I might as well see the architect of my demise.

"Mike!" I stage-whispered. "Wake up! A bear is here!" Mike was only a few feet away, but I could hardly breathe, let alone crawl over to him. My entire body was a rictus of terror.

"Mmmph!" he grumped. "Go back to sleep."

"Mike! Wake up! I think he's eating our food."

He finally flicked on the flashlight and beamed it toward the noises, and I realized I had been mistaken. It wasn't a bear at all — it was two bears. And they were about 15 feet from where I lay rigor-mortising in my bag.

I suppose I have seen bigger creatures in my life — the elephants at the Honolulu Zoo, humpback whales off Lahaina. But I had never seen anything that big that close. Their heads looked like woolly medicine balls. Their bodies were the size of Volkswagens.

"Oh it's just a pair of cubs," Mike said. "Bang the cups together and they'll run away."

"I can't move my arms," I hissed. "I think I'm paralyzed."

My body was paralyzed, but my brain was racing like a lab rat in a treadle wheel. If those shaggy behemoths were indeed "cubs," then they wouldn't have come to our little camp by themselves. They would be with their . . . .

"Look! Up in that tree!" Mike rasped.

12

And there, part-way up the tree to which I had tied the food line, was mama bear. But this wasn't just any mama bear; this was The Mama Bear That Ate Cleveland. Next to her, the baby bears looked like anorexic hamsters.

"Oh God Oh God Oh God Oh God Oh God Oh God!" I chattered.

"Shhhh!" Mike said. "Look, there goes your bear-proof food bag."

Sure enough, with one savage lunge of her paw, mama bear exerted enough force on the tie-off line to send the heavy food sack pinwheeling to the ground. It landed with a thump that must have been music to the baby bears' shoe-sized ears.

"Well, there goes our food," Mike said matter - of - factly, switching off the flashlight. "We might as well go back to sleep." And, amazingly, he did.

As for myself, I knew that I would never sleep again. Even if the bears did let us live through the night — was there enough food in the bag to satisfy them, or would it just be canapes before The Main Course? — I knew that my nights would forever be haunted by the sound of the great mama bear paw lunging at the line.

Once the flashlight was off, other sounds came into focus: the playful shredding of the "rip-stop" nylon food bag, the puncture sounds of fangs on tin, and other odd slurking, chewing and tearing noises as the bears reduced our two-day food supply to spittle and crumbs.

I'll give them this — they didn't bolt their food like some humans I know. They ate as delicately and thoroughly as matrons dispatching watercress sandwiches at a country club tea. And why should the bears hurry their meal? I thought. We were no threat to them — one sleeping human and one wide-awake, quivering, useless shell of a former human.

Finally, after what seemed like hours, the snackling and munching sounds ceased, and the bears padded off into the woods, belching contentedly.

When the gray light of false dawn filtered through the trees, I crept out of my bag and started picking up after the bears. I collected the shredded cans, wrappers, boxes and plastic bottles — all licked clean — the egg shells and gutted stuff sack and burned the whole mess.

In the process, I discovered that the kindly bears had left us some food after all — two florets of broccoli, a small head of cauliflower and a lump of Cheddar cheese the size of a golf ball.

This would be our entire food supply for the next two days, and it all fit snugly into the toe of a sock. During those two days we would hike 25 miles, climbing 2,000 feet out of the canyon on the second day. It was a long, hungry hike, but at least the bears didn't trifle with us again.

Now, when people ask me what backpacking in the Sierras is

like, I can answer in two sentences: "I did that once. The bears ate our food."

Every so often, some weekend woodsman will reply: "Ah, but you should have hung your food in a tree!" I just smile.

— September, 1983

Name That Condo

A fair amount of concern is being voiced in real estate hot tubs these days over an apparent "softening" of Maui's billion-dollar condominium market.

Theories abound. Many blame high interest rates, while some say Realtor Associates are not selling the product aggressively enough. Others have gone so far as to suggest that the Maui condo market may be saturated, what with 14,500 units in place and another 2,000 on the drawing boards.

Nonsense. The only problem with Maui's condominiums is their names.

Names are important, especially now, when 200 nearly-identical Maui condos are vying for buyers, travel agents and tourists. It's not like it used to be in "the old days," back in the early 1970s.

In those far-off times, if a developer wanted to name a project the something-or-other "Kai" or the something-or-other "Shores," he could take justifiable pride in having created something unique and distinctive. The proud buyer of a unit in such a project could boast to friends back home in Edmonton or Moline: "Mildred and I have a unit at the Shores!" And the friends would be suitably impressed.

Not any more. Nowadays the friends, most of them probably Maui condo owners themselves, would simply yawn and ask in bored tones: "Oh really? Which Shores? The Kaanapali Shores? The Menehune Shores? The Polynesian Shores? The Haleakala Shores? The Shores of Maui?"

Let's face facts. There are now a dozen condos called the something-something Shores. The name has lost its cachet. Some of the owners aren't even sure which Shores their unit is in.

The name "Hale" has been abused even more flagrantly. There are now no fewer than 15 Maui condos called the "Hale" something-or-other. Not only do they look alike, to North American ears most of them even sound alike: Hale Kai ... Nani Kai Hale ... Hale Hui Kai ... Hale Kai O Kihei ... Hale Kahekili. Think of all the missed cocktail parties over the years.

"Gee it's been swell meeting you and Howard, Eunice. Why don't you folks join us for drinks this evening at our place? We're in Hale Kai O Kihei 308. Come for sunset, won't you? We have such a lovely sunset."

Shortly before sunset, Eunice and Howard hop into the Corolla and head for . . . where?

"Damn, Eunice — did she say Hale Kai O Kihei or Hale Kahe-Kili? 'Cordin' t'this map here, they're at opposite ends o' th'island!"

"Seems to me she said Hale-Kala-Kihi or Hale-Kihi-Kaio, somethin' like that-there. Is there a Hale-Kala-Kihi on that list? Oh, look, the sun's goin' down."

You get the idea. Twelve Shores, 15 Hales, 17 Kais, 10 Beaches, 8 Sands, 8 Resorts, 7 Royals, 6 Villas and hosts of Bays, Gardens, Villages, Terraces, Manors and Townhouses, not to mention Sunrises, Sunsets, Kuleanas, Paniolos and Menehunes.

There must be a master list somewhere, one of those three-column jobs where you combine "any word from column A" with any words from B and C to come up with the desired condo name:

Column A	Column B	Column C
Hale	Kai	Townhouses
Kihei	Alii	Villas
Napili	Nani	Village
Lahaina	Kane	Vista
Honokowai	Nalu	Estates
Kahana	Bay	Shores
Wailea	Koa	Terrace
Kapalua	Beach	Gardens
Hana	Sunset	Ridge
Kaanapali	Surf	Kuleana
Kamaole	Lani	Resort
Maui	Paniolo	Elua Phase II
Maalaea	Hui	Ekolu Phase III

With names like these, is it any wonder Maui's condos aren't selling? The 1981 market is, after all, a highly sophisticated market. We're not talking Ma and Pa Kettle these days. We're talking buyers who can spend as much as $750,000 for the privilege of owning a unit on beautiful, prestigious, one-of-a-kind Maui.

The least Maui could do is come up with some beautiful, prestigious, one - of - a - kind names for those expensive units. Perhaps:

Name That Condo

Column A	Column B	Column C
Ultimate	Black Velvet	Hideaway
Exquisite	Bejeweled	Retreat
International	Jet Set	Heaven-On-Earth
Billionaire	Champagne	Republic
Bo Derek	Silken	Shangri-La
Robert Redford	Five-Star	Extravaganza
Exclusive	Sapphire	Hanging Gardens
Mink-Lined	Starlight	Taj Mahal
Sophia Loren	Caviar	Getaway
Bjorn Borg	Lear Jet	Beulah Land
Intimate	Cocaine	Grotto
Gilt-Edged	Ferrari	Never-Never-Land
Prince Charles	Drambuie	Cathedral

That should do for starters. After you've worked out all the combinations and permutations, why don't you join us for drinks this evening? We're in Intimate Lear Jet Shangri-La 308.

We have such a lovely sunset.

—August, 1981

Waiting in Line

It was a hectic Friday afternoon in Kahului, and there were lines all over town.

Lines of people stood in the banks, at the post office, at the checkout counters of markets and stores. Long lines of cars and trucks formed at the major intersections and at the drive-up windows of fast-food restaurants. Later, there would be lines for the movies and for the shows at the hotels.

In every line, the fine art of waiting in Hawaii could be observed. No pushing or shoving. No honking of horns. No fist fights.

Just . . . waiting.

As the pace of island life accelerates, and the demand for goods and services grows, knowing how to wait can be a very important skill. Those who don't know how to wait can go crazy here. Those who know how to wait may go crazy, too — but it will take longer.

For most island people, waiting is no big thing. Many have a capacity for it that borders on being genetic — perhaps the legacy of ancestors who toiled patiently in fishing and farming villages where life was governed by the unalterable rhythms of nature.

Things can get tricky, though, for visitors and new residents who come to Hawaii from fast-paced metropolitan areas where the failure of the 5:06 to depart at 5:06 causes blood vessels to burst in the commuters' foreheads.

In that competitive "time is money" environment, waiting is not viewed as a natural condition of life, but as a thing to be avoided at all costs — and to be resented bitterly when it does occur.

In order to ease the former metropolitan's transition to "Hawaiian time," *The Maui News* offers the following tips:

— When waiting for service in isle stores or restaurants, try to remain calm. Do not threaten employees or demand to see the manager. Avoid big city expressions like "What's the delay here?" and "I'm paying good money for this!" Such utterances will only make you anxious and increase your waiting time, for the length of a wait in Hawaii is directly proportional to the anxiety of the person waiting.

— When ordering goods or having work performed, remember to use expressions like: "No rush," "Whenever," and "I'll check back next month." Smile pleasantly as you stroll out the door, as though you have all the time in the world. You do.

— If you enjoy reading in lines, keep a book handy, especially when making payday transactions at the bank. *War and Peace, Hawaii* or *Decline and Fall of the Roman Empire* should get you from the end of the line to the teller's cage on a normal Friday. During holiday season, *Webster's Third New International* is recommended.

— While waiting in Maui traffic jams, attend to personal hygiene chores that may have been neglected at home. Clip nails, shave legs and underarms, or trim unwanted ear hair. Keep soapy water and sponges handy for rush hour "driving" in Lahaina or Upcountry, where it is often possible to wash your car before the line moves again.

— While waiting at the post office with your head lowered politely, notice the feet of the other people in line. Try to imagine what they do for a living. At the market, study the food in others' carts. Learn to differentiate bagoong, won bok and bok choy. Imagine eating these foods.

— When waiting at a "fast" food restaurant, try to remember how grandma's cooking used to taste at family gatherings. If this doesn't work, imagine faraway places like Bangkok or Mauritania. How do the people live in those places? What kinds of fast food do they have?

— If you are waiting in an air-conditioned line, think about how hot it is outside. If you are waiting in a hot line, imagine faraway places like Bangkok or Mauritania.

— If you must think while waiting, do not think of all the other things you should be doing, as this will only make you anxious and lengthen your wait, as discussed earlier. Instead, think how lucky you are to be standing in line instead of selling solar panels.

— Above all, remember that you are in Hawaii, where waiting is as much a part of life as a second job or a $30 bag of groceries. Learn to enjoy waiting. You're going to be doing a lot of it.

— June, 1981

Greenhouse Effect

Hot? Did you say it's hot out there?

You bet it's hot — and not just because this is September. Something weird is happening to the weather.

On TV the other week, Walter Cronkite talked about the "greenhouse effect." He said the Earth is heating up as an ever-thickening blanket of carbon dioxide spewed from cars and smokestacks acts like a greenhouse to trap reflected sunlight.

Big deal, you say — what's that got to do with the price of Canadian real estate?

Nothing ... yet. But as the atmosphere heats up, the polar ice caps will begin to melt. There's a lot of ice in those caps — the one in Antarctica alone is a mile thick and 2,000 miles across. If that starts to go, keep your Churchills handy.

As the ice dissolves, Cronkite said, the sea level could rise 50 feet or more in the next few decades, putting a lot of interesting places under water and radically altering world weather patterns.

The Los Angeles Times recently speculated that North American rain patterns may change: "As the rain moves north, Canada would become warm and possibly lush, an agricultural paradise. But the corn belt of the American midlands would revert to the Dust Bowl days of the 1930s, and the U.S. ... could become a country scratching for international crumbs."

There it is: Canada would become "warm and possibly lush," a "paradise," while America turns into a "dust bowl."

Friends, the time to buy Canadian real estate is now!

That fabulous country, the second largest expanse of tundra on Earth, has long been dismissed as a frozen wasteland fit only for grizzlies and Mounties. But those days are over. Thanks to carbon dioxide, Canada is in for some much-needed improvements.

As Canada's weather heats up, tropical fruits and flowers will bloom where only lichens can survive today. The country's many glaciers will become warm - water lakes, luring dust - blinded Americans north to the lush new resorts of Moose Jaw, Snag and Stony Rapids. The lonely howling of timber wolves will give way to the soothing clip-clip of yardboys trimming bougainvillea hedges.

Friends, the greenhouse effect is going to make Canada THE vacation spot of the 2000s. But don't tell the Canadians. They're still buying up beachfront property on Maui, little realizing that it's going to be growing limu by the time the second mortgage is paid off.

Once the sea level rises 50 feet, surfers will be catching waves on the roof of Menehune Shores, and Wailea will be a "world-class resort" for moray eels. Let's face it: Maui's days as a paradise are numbered. Once those ice caps go, few will want to vacation in a place where the ocean laps gently on the shores of Waikapu Dump.

Canada, on the other hand, will be a Maui-style paradise very soon — and that means gold neck chains and a matched set of Afghans for those shrewd enough to get in on the ground floor.

Interested? We knew you would be. We're Time Share Canada, and we're ready to deal.

We are now offering — to a select handful of very discriminating investors — our "Canadian Tundralands" package of time share specials in the Yukon and Northwest Territories. For just $179.99 per month, you can own a "vacation for life" in the thrilling Yukon, home of the 1897 Gold Rush and site of Carmacks, Teslin and Pelly Crossing, with its pulse-pounding nightlife and riotous Vole Stampede.

Or perhaps your tastes run more to the peaceful Northwest Territories — scenic MacKenzie District with its Great Slave Lake and Grizzly Bear Mountains; tranquil Keewatin District, with fewer than two people per square mile; unhurried Franklin District, with no people per square mile.

Resales? Glad you asked. Once the world realizes what's happening to itself, you won't be able to buy a Canadian vacation for all the gold in the Klondike. And that means those who buy Canadian Tundralands time shares right now will multiply their investments a hundredfold by the time you finish reading this sentence.

Why be left out? Mail your first $179.99 installment today to: Canadian Tundralands, 2nd Lean-to Past Tuktoyaktuk's Hutch, Port Radium, Northwest Territories, 01. You'll be mighty glad you did.

— September, 1981

Christmas Calendars

I see by my Sierra Club appointment calendar that it's Dec. 22 — time to start the Christmas shopping.

The calendar made me think of this as much as the date. Calendars make useful gifts, especially if you get "behind" at Christmas, as I do, and have to shop defensively.

When shopping defensively, I usually go to a nearby place and buy many units of the same thing. One year it was Darth Vader soap bars from Craft's. One year everybody got hanafuda cards from Toda Drug. Last year's generic gift was corduroy footballs in school colors.

That's what I call "preemptive strike" shopping — where you lay down a strafing run of small, quick-hitting presents and then streak for cover. It's good to be far away when the gifts are opened and compared, and everybody realizes they got the same thing. If you're close up, as with the immediate family on Christmas morning, it's good not to give everyone the same thing.

I'll never forget my parents and grandmother gazing in dismay at their coal-black Vader soap bars — just holding them loosely on their laps and not knowing what to say. And I don't think Uncle Dave ever has used his hanafuda cards.

Some years the relatives get to puzzle over things I make myself — stapled booklets of articles, crude block prints stamped from carved potatoes, photographs of dark, artsy scenes. These gifts generally embarrass the family, who once hoped I would find a nice job in a bank.

But at least those presents were made, bought and disbursed by Christmas. This year I waited too long. Presents have arrived for me, and I have no presents to give back. This may be my calendar year.

Calendars make good defensive gifts, because you can slip them to the recipients the week after Christmas without terminal guilt. Since they don't kick in anyway until January, calendars aren't so much late Christmas presents as early New Year presents. And they slide right into the mail — perfect for Mainland giftees who otherwise might expect something thoughtful and expensive in a box.

Some people scoff at calendars, but I find them indispensable. Ever since the rats got my watch — the one that gave the day of the week — I keep a calendar handy at all times. I've found that people are pretty impressed when I know what day it is.

If someone calls me here at the office, for instance, I just flick my eyes to the calendar as I speak. "Gosh, it's great to hear from you on a Thursday, Dec. 17, Ed. How's the family?"

Or if someone wants his people to power lunch with my people, I'll say: "Well, this is Tuesday; how does Friday look for your people? Dairy Queen at noon?" It makes an impression.

Besides giving the day and the date, calendars can enhance your machismo at work, putting your bosses and colleagues on notice that you are a fiery young stallion on the way up, a force to be reckoned with.

As a force more likely to be reckoned without, I use calendars to cover my frequent, prolonged absences on volleyball days or when the surf's up. I had to do this because my employers kept asking: "Do you work here, or do you just come in to use the phone?"

Now, before I go surfing, I churn paperwork all over my desk and lay the Sierra Club appointment calendar on top. Using pens with different color inks, I scribble in powerful, tightly-spaced appointments for each day: "Yoko, noon, Kapalua . . . Gorbachev, 12:45, Wailea . . . Gen. Haig, 1:30, Country Club."

I pencil in weekend and holiday jobs as well, because off-hours work is honored in this business. Nothing too pleasant, though: perhaps "sewage treatment tour" for a sunny Saturday, or "investigate orphan home tragedy" for Christmas Eve. If it looks like the surf is going to hold for several days, I "cover Afghan conflict."

None of this would be possible without the Sierra Club desk-top appointment calendar, the one with a wilderness photo on each facing page. At $7.95 a pop, the Sierra calendar is too costly for me to disburse in bulk this year, but I will be happy to receive one.

— December, 1987

Skiing Bozo

When my brother Mike invited me to go skiing in California this spring, I'm afraid I wasn't very receptive. That's because I had tried the sport on the East Coast 20 years before, and I was still shivering.

Skiing back there meant driving many hours to the upper reaches of New England, where a range of dismal little mountains offered packed snow, sub-zero temperatures and winds that cut like a machete. There was a certain terrifying exhilaration, I'll admit, in streaking out of control down icy runs at Mad River Glen and Mount Snow, but it wasn't my idea of a swell time. The discomfort level was too high, my pain threshold too low.

The only part of the whole experience that appealed to me was the "apres-ski" component. Wind-blinded, ears and fingers burning, I would stagger into the lodge at dusk, wipe my nose on the backs of my gloves, and collapse into a chair near the fire.

Strong drink was required to restore basic motor functions, and several toddies eventually brought on a semblance of well-being. But even then, the pleasure of the "apres-ski" was proportional to the ordeal of the "ski."

Put another way, the pleasure of not hitting yourself on the head with a hammer isn't much ... but it can approach orgasmic intensity when you've been hitting yourself on the head with a hammer.

I finally gave my skis, poles and boots to some hardy Yankee and went back to sitting indoors, daydreaming about Hawaii. I found I could be as miserable doing that as I could skiing, and it was a lot cheaper.

Then, two decades later, I went skiing again. The mitten was flung down by my brother Mike, an intrepid Californian who previously had tested my mettle on a pair of backpacking expeditions involving hungry bears and inflatable boats.

This time Mike informed me that he had purchased a partnership for the winter in a "ski cabin" at a place called Donner Lake, a mere snowball's throw from the famous Lake Tahoe ski areas of Squaw Valley and Alpine Meadows. Would I like to go skiing?

"Would I like to throw myself under a train?" I replied. "Would I like to slap a pit bull? No, I'll sit this one out. Drop me a card from the intensive care unit."

Of course I ended up going over there. It was fun.

The most fun was riding on the chair lifts. These ingenious devices carry skiers from the base of the mountain to the various "runs" along its crest and flanks. On a sunny day, you don't want to get off the lift.

The chairs seat two or three abreast in upholstered comfort and clank along at a pleasant pace high above the ground. From this lofty perch, it was possible to see snow-flocked forests, granite crags and the piercing blue of the High Sierra sky.

"How beautiful!" I murmured, watching the tiny figures of advanced skiers zigzag across a distant bowl. Others zipped beneath the chair lift, slicing hissing S's in the crisp snow.

About midway through the chair ride, we glided over a Swiss chalet sort of affair crowded with skiers. They were laughing and eating sandwiches and quaffing steins of beer. A forest of skis and poles poked up through the snowbanks nearby, and the sunny deck was alive with wholesome-looking women in braids.

"Let's go there!" I cried. "Look at those women!"

"No!" my brother said, pulling me back onto the seat. "We're here to ski. There are women on Maui."

"Not with braids," I whined. But it was too late — our "chairavan" had left the sunny little chalet behind, and now we were clanking upward past silent forests, circling hawks and steep, snow-choked ravines. The ground looked very far away.

"When do the little oxygen masks drop down?" I asked.

"Relax," Mike said. "We're not even at 10,000 feet. Look behind us."

Turning in the chair, I beheld Lake Tahoe, a flawless tourmaline set in a ring of shining mountains. It looked like *The Far Pavilions.*

"Let's go there!" I said.

"Not now we don't," he said. "It's very cold out on that lake. It's so deep that there are bodies from 60 years ago, still perfectly preserved, lying on the bottom."

"Yes, it is nice right here on these slopes," I agreed, turning away from the lake. A wooden structure appeared up ahead of us. "What's that, another chalet?"

"That's the lift station where we get off," he said. "Raise your ski tips and lean forward in the chair. When we're on the ramp, stand up."

The next thing I knew, our skis bumped up onto a narrow, snow-covered platform which soon began falling away beneath us.

25

"Now!" Mike said. Pushing himself up off the seat, he glided easily down the ramp. I gulped, hesitated, and lunged forward.

Suddenly, I was skiing down the ramp!

Suddenly, I was not skiing down the ramp.

Like a crippled imperial walker from "Star Wars," I helicoptered wildly for a moment, grabbed at a railing and went down, skis and poles clashing metallically. I tumbled to a stop just as the next two skiers ejected from their chair. They were on me in a flash, and soon three of us were thrashing in the snow, skis and limbs entangled.

"Stay down!" my brother shouted as the second chair whipped past, inches from my head. I glanced back up the ramp in time to see two more bodies hurtling toward the pile-up. Someone shrieked. There was impact and cursing. Things were getting out of control.

The lift operator stopped the chairs and came out of the little house to sort through the rubble. With her help, we finally gained our feet and moved off, the others glaring at me over their shoulders. I pretended I was back on Maui, doing a crossword puzzle in the Chart House bar.

"Nice work," my brother grinned. "And that was just the ramp. I can't wait to see you out on the hill."

"Hill" is not the word I would have used to describe the thing we now stood on the brink of. Hills are round, friendly little places suitable for picnics and kite-flying. This was a death-chute.

"I'm riding back down on the chair," I said, bending over to unlatch my bindings. "See you at the little chalet."

"Nice try, Timmy Bozo," Mike said. "You can only ride the chair down if you're hurt."

It was a classic Catch-22. If I skiied down I would be killed ... but my remains could ride down in the chair. I was pondering this when I felt a hand push me forward.

"Heeeeere we go!" Mike said cheerfully.

"Maaaaama!" I screamed, but I was years too late.

Down the white death-chute we flew. As my skis hissed over the snow, I tried to recall the formula for acceleration. Was it acceleration equals mass times velocity? If so, I was in trouble, for I had eaten well that morning. Omelets, blueberry pancakes, hash browns, sausages. Lots of mass.

Things were happening quickly. Other skiers flashed by, looking relaxed and confident. A row of trees flashed by, looking big and solid. The piney air stung my cheeks like aftershave.

Further downslope, Mike slalomed from side to side, planting his poles and turning smoothly around them, his weight always downhill, his skis in perfect parallel. Body erect, knees slightly bent, he was a marvel of speed and snake-hipped agility. After 15 years of skiing, he had become One With The Mountain.

I, too, became one with the mountain, but it only took me 15 seconds. I remember a fleeting glimpse of the distant lake, a quick pan of the sky, a close-up of one ski tip crossing over the other. Then everything went white. There was a blissful moment of free fall followed by impact as I reentered Earth's gravitational field. I became a one-man avalanche, tumbling and clattering downhill like something ejected at high speed from a trash compactor.

I finally skidded to a stop on my belly, skis hopelessly entangled, my arms outstretched. I lay like that for some time, breathing, intent on milking the scene for its dramatic possibilities. I pretended I was "The Man Who Skiied Down Everest."

"Great fall!" my brother shouted. "You didn't even lose your skis!"

Indeed . . . they were still attached to my legs, which were still attached to my body. I could see my arms out in front of me, so I knew my head was still attached, too. Amazingly, I didn't hurt. That would come later.

"That was fun!" I grunted, ratcheting my skis around. "I want to do that again!"

"I'm sure you will, Timmy Bozo," he said. "But first let's run through the 'snowplow' one more time."

Ah, yes. The "snowplow." How could I have forgotten this simple survival stance — body in a fetal crouch, arms akimbo, knees bent inward, ski tips angled toward each other?

Planting my poles in the slope uphill, I heaved myself onto my feet. Then Mike demonstrated the snowplow, showing how a transfer of body weight from one ski to the other would enable me to make primitive turns and thus control my rate of descent.

The poles, which I had flapped like ailerons on my initial run, are supposed to be stabbed into the ground alternately as the skier courses downhill, he explained. Planting a pole below and to one side of the skis causes the torso to swivel downhill, thus "unweighting" the uphill ski, which can then be swung around easily to become the downhill ski. Something like that.

"Lean, plant, swivel, unweight, turn," he coached. "That's all you have to remember. Got it?"

"Cake," I said. "I'll race you to the little chalet. Give me a 40-day head start."

We pushed off again, and soon Mike was flying over moguls and slashing through the deep powder that lay in pockets between stands of pines. The sun winked on his poles as he flicked off down the hill.

I crept downward in my hunched snowplow position, scrabbling across the flank of the hill like a hermit crab, then turning wildly and scrabbling across in the other direction. "Lean, plant, swivel, unweight, turn!" I cried, executing a "snowplow turn" without great bodily harm.

Just then a wholesome figure in braids shot past, and my attention began to drift. "Lean, plant, unweight, turn, swivel! ... Unweight, turn, plant, swivel and lean!" More braids. "Turn, swivel ... plant?"

There was a fleeting glimpse of the distant lake, a quick pan of the sky, a close-up of ski tips crossing . . . .

After several more spills, I modified my technique to "Stand up, close your eyes, go like hell!" It wasn't classically pure, but I enjoyed the sensation of speed, and I found that I could control my descent simply by crash-diving to the side whenever I got going too fast.

This kamikaze method worked well as long as I skiied "intermediate" slopes like Weasel and Sherwood Forest, but at the end of the day all the skiers on the mountain had to go down something called the "Valley Run."

This was a steep, narrow road in the snow into which all the other ski runs funneled. Roughly two miles long, it snaked from the mid-mountain lift stations to the main ski lodge at the head of the parking lot.

For accomplished Tahoe-area skiers, the Valley Run is the perfect ending to a vigorous day on the slopes — a long, fast glide with a full view of the lake and the fellowship of hundreds of happy companions.

To a displaced Maui skier, it was a different kettle of ice entirely. I called it the "Valley of the Shadow of Death Run," because I feared some evil.

"OK, we're going down the Valley Run now," my brother said solemnly. "Your kamikaze style won't work on this one. It's too steep, and there are too many other people. Just stay in the snowplow and take your time. I'll look out for you."

As we stood at the crest of that final run, I gazed out upon God's white earth. Most of the mountain was in shadow, but the highest peaks burned with a clean, gold fire. The sky beyond them ached with color. The forests were dark and still. A full moon floated over the lake.

I didn't want to leave.

"Time to go, Timmy," Mike said. We pushed off and were soon hurtling down the snow freeway with hundreds of other skiers, some white-haired, some barely out of kindergarten, all more skillful than I. This was good, because they could anticipate my motor spasms and swerve around me.

"Passing on your right!" they would call before rocketing past, or "Watch out to the left!" But nobody snarled: "Use the chairlift, flatlander!" I was grateful for that.

Locked into a rigid fearplow, I skirted the sheer dropoffs on the downhill side of the run. Were those ravines littered with the bleached skeletons of other beginners, I wondered, their tattered parkas lifting in the breeze? I leaned, planted, swiveled, unweighted and turned. Funny how those little skills come back when your life is flashing before your eyes.

Finally, shaky but happy, we reached the main ski lodge at the base of the mountain. The restaurant and the huge indoor bar roared with apres-ski festivity. A disco dance was going on, too, but Mike and I carried our Irish coffees outside to the deserted deck.

"So this is what skiing is all about," I mused, watching the last bright peaks flame out, one by one.

"Beats walking," he said.

— May, 1984

Sand and Rocks

So, what is the difference between sand and rocks, anyway?

This pivotal issue has seized the attention of *The Maui News* readers, fired their imaginations and bucked up their fighting spirit as no other since jet skis.

Pithy, pungent commentaries have appeared in our pages weekly since the Maui County Council ruled in its serene wisdom that Wailea's Polo Beach is "rocky" rather than "sandy" so that a hotel could be built closer to the ocean there.

One man wrote that "sand is small and white; rocks are big and black," and this column cannot improve on that. Nor can it state the case more eloquently than did the writer who compared the county council to the deluded monarch in "The Emperor's New Clothes."

Yet it is curious to me that the rockiness of this bleak, foreboding shoreline — this mariners' graveyard of bleached bones and broken ships — has for so long escaped our attention.

County officials are blameless, since most have not been to the shore since childhood. These people are golfers, not beachgoers. But you would think that the real estate mavens and the resort developers — usually so astute in telling sand from rock — would have realized by now the enormity of their error.

Here they've been selling millionaire mansions, condos and luxury hotel rooms on the premise that Polo "Beach" is sandy — and the millionaires have been snapping them up, hoping no doubt to play polo on that very beach one fine day.

Imagine their surprise when the English nanny brings little Muffy and Skippy home from the children's first outing at Polo Beach.

"Mummy, Mummy!" Skippy shrieks, staggering across the porte cochere, his little body a mass of welts and gashes, his hip crushed, one eye rolled back.

"Lovey, don't touch Mummy now, you'll stain my caftan. Why, just look at you! I send you children with Nanny to play in the sand, and you come home looking like this. Stay off the Persian rug!"

"Mummy!" wails little Muffy, as splattered as one of her parents' Jackson Pollocks. "There was no sand, Mummy! No sand at all! Just

30

wicked, wicked rocks everywhere! And we had to play in them!"

"Well, I never! How could there be no sand at the beach? Your father and I should have listened to that county council in the first place. Jeeves, pack our things. We're moving to Kapalua."

In the next mansion over, a similar tragedy unfolds as a billionaire industrialist staggers from his chauffeured Rolls, his riding clothes in tatters, the shattered grip of a polo mallet clutched in one gloved hand.

His Parisian mistress greets him at the door, her exquisite mouth forming an attractive moue of alarm. "Oooh, Bucky, qu'est-ce qui happen to you, ma cher?"

"Damn!" he shouts, flinging his splintered mallet. "Nastiest chukkar I've ever played. Had to put three horses down, and we lost Sir Rodney and the Sheik as well. Polo 'Beach' indeed! There's more sand in an hourglass. Pack your nightie, my sweet. We're moving to Kohala Ranch."

Yes, it could happen here. If one beach can go to rock in a single county council meeting, there's no telling where this thing could end. While the crisis seems limited at this point to beaches where world-class hotels are to be built, even that covers a lot of sand ... or rock, as the case may be.

What about Kaanapali's idyllic North Beach, where six world-class hotels are to rise? Or Lanai's stunning "White Manele," or the Kaluakoi coast of Molokai? All had wide, soft, sandy beaches the last time I looked, but with new hotels coming in, there's no guarantee they'll stay that way.

So, what is the difference between sand and rocks?

I don't know. But if a developer tells the council that a beach is rocky — and the council votes that the beach is rocky — then for God's sake don't send your children there or try to play polo on it.

This warning isn't just for Maui's world-class millionaires. We plain folk who simply fish, surf, swim and pick limu, who walk the sands at evening and in the cool of dawn, must be ever vigilant, lest the council change all our beaches to black rock, too.

Have you checked your beach lately?

— May, 1988

Couch Potato

It was a nice rainy Sunday in Kuau — the kind where the rain falls for a while, blows on by, then returns later as you're pushing the lawn mower out to the yard. "Good excuse" rain, I call it.

Casting a sorrowful eye skyward, you announce that this one seems to be here to stay.

"Seems to be here to stay," you grumble, stamping around some. "Look, the whole yard's getting soaked!" Then, unlacing your boots with a sigh: "Might as well watch the game . . . ."

Some days it's a good idea just to lie around and do nothing. Many societies value this practice, but it's hard to justify in ours. We have a double standard in America — lie around and watch TV, but let the TV scold you for it.

I got a good tongue-lashing from my little set Sunday afternoon. The Raiders and the 49ers were heaving each other around Candlestick Park in some meaningless encounter, but I was happy. Rain pelted the windows as I lay atop my bed like a cartoon hobo, awash in Sunday papers. I browsed on a half-read trash novel (*The Delta Decision*) and a half-eaten package of Hilo Cremes.

Suddenly an angry voice snapped at me from the television. A yuppie woman in workout clothes, her face sharp and beaded with sweat, glared at me so fiercely that I thought we must have known each other in the past.

"Listen, whatever it was, I'm really sorry . . ." I stammered, but the yuppie woman cut me off.

"What's it going to be today?" she challenged, her voice snapping like a locker room towel. "Aerobics?"

"No!" I said.

"Weight lifting?"

"No!" I cried. "Nothing heavier than a Hilo Creme."

But she ripped on, fists planted defiantly on her hips, static electricity crackling from her hair. "Bicycling? Running? Gymnastics? Handball? Volleyball? Fencing?" Her voice was like tearing fabric.

"Look, it's raining here!" I said. "So cut it out!"

She pushed her sweaty face even closer to the camera, and I

jerked backward instinctively. Her eyes were gray and steely, and you could have struck sparks off her smile. "What's it going to be today?" she repeated.

"Oh, I think I'll have the coconut chiffon cheesecake and the Kahlua torte," I began, but a chorus of angry voices shouted me down.

"Aerobics! Weight lifting! Bicycling! Running! Gymnastics! Volleyball!" the voices chanted. Images of bouncing shoes and twisting torsos crossed the screen. The effect was as chilling as the demonic chorus from "Carmina Burana."

The ad slammed to a close after one final glare from the yuppie woman. "Just do it!" she commanded. There was a heavy, booming sound like a great stone door closing forever, and the screen went to black. The name of a U.S. nuclear missile — "Nike" — flashed briefly in white and was gone.

The whole thing had lasted perhaps 20 seconds, but I was deeply shaken. My heart pounded, a light sweat broke out on my upper lip, and several eyebrow hairs turned white. What was this? I wondered — aerobics from hell? Jane Fonda for Republicans?

The rain beat on the walls like a guilty conscience. To a newly minted couch potato like myself, the ad's premise was stark. It didn't even ask if its viewers were going to take up some grueling, self-abnegating physical challenge that afternoon: that much was assumed. The question was, which one would it be?

Personally, with the exception of volleyball, I found the list of choices a little severe. "Lying in bed eating Hilo Cremes" wasn't on the list, I noticed, and neither was "reading trash novels and listening to the rain."

The ad's final, fleeting reference to the U.S. nuclear missile was also troubling. After some effort, I gained my feet, staggered manfully across my room and wobbled off down the hall in search of housemates. The flashing pinpoints of colored light preceding me indicated how long it had been since I walked.

One of the housemates was in the living room, watching her giant TV. I asked her if she'd seen the aerobics-from-hell ad. She nodded. "Well, what is that 'Nike' at the end?" I asked. "Isn't Nike a missile?"

"It's a sports shoe," she laughed. "You either don't work out, or you don't watch enough TV."

It was a tough choice.

— November, 1988

33

Talking Cars

My mom showed me her new car recently. It was a nice-looking silver car — some kind of Datsun station wagon, if I recall. It had power windows, power steering and a music system that makes my car stereo sound like forklifts fighting in an alley.

These features pleased my mom, but they weren't what convinced her to buy the car. She bought the car because it talks.

"Listen to this," she said proudly. Leaving the key in the ignition, she opened the door, as though going off on an errand.

"The key is in the ignition," the car said in a feminine voice. Its tone was pleasant but authoritative, like a receptionist for a prosperous law firm. A bell chimed softly, and the message was repeated in the same tone.

That voice enabled the Datsun to prevail over three or four other station wagons my mom was considering, and it also sold her best friend on the car. "I took Adelaide for a spin the day I got it," she said. "And when she heard the car talk, she just fell in love with it. The very next day she traded in her big Mercury and bought a little wagon just like mine."

"Does hers have the same voice?" I asked.

"Exactly the same," my mom said. "I think they only have the one voice."

This didn't trouble her at all, but the more I thought about it, the more it seemed to me that the car companies were missing out on a good thing. I mean, they make cars in every conceivable style and color, offer various kinds of engines, tires, stereos, hubcaps, upholstery and so on — why not offer a choice of voices?

Women might like a car with a Tom Selleck or Frank Sinatra voice, and I'll bet men car buyers would go for something in a sultry Diana Ross or a pouty Christy Brinkley. The Merle Haggard or Loretta Lynn voice would be a hit with country music fans, and golfers could have an Arnold Palmer voice remind them to change their Pennzoil regularly.

The possibilities are limitless. With a little creativity, you could even tailor the voices to the cars. Imagine strolling up to a white-on-white Cadillac Coupe De Ville with tinted windows, gangster whitewalls and twin TV antennas in the back. Opening the door and sliding across the powder blue calfskin upholstery, you insert the key into the ignition.

"Hey, wha's happenin', Homes?" the car rumbles in a deep Mr. T voice. "Now, I don't wanna mess wif yo mind, but I gots to hip you to dis rat now — you done lef' yo' key in my switch. 'Taint no big thing, Clyde, but if you split now, you gon' have to call The Man when you get back, 'cause I be stolen. Dig you later, fool."

On a visit to a sports car dealership, you might encounter a ruby red Ferrari with velvet upholstery and a Gina Lollobrigida voice.

"Bona Sera, amore," the car whispers huskily. "You forgetta something, beeg boy? You know I love when you switcha me on, cara mia, but if you leavea you key in here, I'll be someone else's bambina. Then you'll have to go backa to your Fiat. Ciao."

A midnight black half-ton pickup with roll bar, four-foot-tall studded tires and optional attack Dobermans might greet you this way:

"Howzit, bool? Get bodz? Eh, we go cruise Front Shtreet tonight. I like spock dat sassy red Stingray weet da beeg slicks. Befo' we holo-holo, I gotta tal you somteen, bot. Da key stay eensi' da dakine. Eef you go walk away now, poho fo' you, bruddah, cuz I goin' end op down Mud Flats, shtreep to da reemz. Latuhz, brah."

For the moment, these car voices only concern themselves with keys and gas and seat belts, and they're only available in new cars. I'm grateful for that. I'd hate to hear what my car would say if it could talk:

"You banana! You call this maintenance? Look at this rusted-out body! Listen to this wheezing engine! I burn out my valves for you, and what do I get? An oil change twice a year, if I'm lucky. And do I ever get a bath and a nice wax job? Nooooo — you're too busy surfing and being late for work. And what about this front end shimmy? Where are those oil filters you promised? And another thing . . . ."

On second thought, my mom can have her talking car. I think I'll just listen to the radio.

— January, 1984

Rust

My old bodysurfing pal Wally was out in front of Ooka's the other evening stringing a tow-rope from one of his trucks to the other. The operable truck was nothing special — a white, late-model pickup with lumber racks. It was the other one that caught my eye. That one was a Rembrandt of rust.

Originally a 1979 silver Ford Courier, the vehicle was now a Maui Saltair — and the salt air was taking it back, crumb by oxidized crumb. Wally had little trouble finding holes to loop the tow-rope through; the trick was finding solid metal between the holes.

Rust had streaked the truck's flanks brown and had chewed up the chassis like recoiless rifle fire. Through some of the larger holes, I watched a family walking along the other side of the street. I realized I had never looked through a truck before.

Admiring Wally's Ford reminded me — new car hoopla to the contrary — that we in Hawaii never really "own" our vehicles. They are only on loan to us from the environment for shorter or longer periods of time. In Paukukalo, where Wally's trucks live, it's usually a short-term loan.

Paukukalo is the home of rust, the place where rust begins and ends its day. Situated at the very pommel of Maui's windy "saddle," the little town with the poi factory, the Iglesia Ni Cristo church and the weathered Shinto mission catches more salt spray in the face than Dennis Connor.

Except for the heavily Bondoed cars parked along its seaward-facing streets, a stroll through Paukukalo is like a visit to a pre-metallic Hawaii, because nothing metallic can survive there very long.

Rust didn't have a whole lot to do in pre-metallic Hawaii, because there weren't any 10-speed bikes or electric can openers lying around. Rust's only job in those days was to turn the dirt red. Then Captain Cook brought iron to the islands, and rust said: "Kaukau!"

It was tough going for rust in those early years, because even though metal had arrived, it was mostly big metal — cannons and

36

cannon balls, whalers' try pots and anchors, sturdy thwart pins and the like. Even the nails of the day were massive enough to give rust a toothache.

The Industrial Revolution was some help, because even though most of the main industrial stuff like boilers and tram cars remained heavy-gauge, the invention of moving parts ensured a constant supply of smaller, lighter-gauge pieces for rust pupu.

The big break for Hawaii-based rust came in the early years of the 20th century, when the mass production techniques pioneered by Henry Ford sent the first battalions of what would become a mighty army of replicable metal objects clinking and whirring toward their doom in the islands.

Soon there were enough seized-up electric shavers, push lawn mowers and rowing machines to feed a rust family "baby luau" at Hale Nanea, and it wasn't long before mischievous rust youngsters stole into island closets to hanger-stain favorite aloha shirts.

Automobiles had long since replaced tram cars by World War II, but they did not become Hawaii rust's favorite food until the tank-like Hudsons and Packards of the John Wayne era gave way to the zippy, rice paper-thin compacts of the John Travolta years.

These so-called "economy" cars are a paradox here — while they are long on gas mileage, there is so little chassis left after the first few years that they can scarcely mount a respectable collision, let alone match Blue Book.

But these cars are easy to attach tow ropes to, and if you look through the larger holes in their sides, you can sometimes see the rust family walking cheerfully toward Paukukalo.

— *October, 1987*

Mid-Life Crisis

It was a sign of mid-life something. I was out bodysurfing Middle Lefts recently when my contemporary, Vince, paddled up.

The swell wasn't that big — inconsistent four to six feet — but both of us were sucking more wind that we like to admit. We rested for a minute, a midlife island in a sea of steely young surf commandos with restless eyes and pointy boards. There were dozens of them.

"Who are all these guys?" I puffed. "Shouldn't they be in school, or in the Army or something?"

"These are all the guys who used to be 13," Vince said. "Now they're 17 and hungry for surf."

"And we're the guys who used to be 17," I laughed. "Only now we're 41."

A set came through, so Vince and I said "see you" and did our best to avoid impalement by the younger generation, already slashing their way toward surfer immortality.

"Too many young guys out," I grumped, thrashing for the bottom as a pack of thrusters sliced by overhead. Later, driving back to work, I realized I hadn't said "too many guys out," but "too many young guys out." I knew then that I had become "older."

It steals up on you, this aging business. One day you're a surfing immortal, the next day you're fishing your dentures out of a bedside water glass. I'm somewhere in the middle, about the point where my dad was when he switched to boxer shorts and started taking naps. My brother Mike and I couldn't believe it.

"Do you think her's sick?" Mike asked with 9-year-old concern.

"Sleeping sickness," I said. "Tsetse fly got him in the war. It hits every afternoon about the same time. He just has to sleep it off."

"Is that why he has to wear sandals now?" Mike asked.

"Yeah, he has to," I said sadly. "Boxer shorts, too, and glasses for reading."

"Poor Dad," Mike said. "I hope we never get it."

We held out for 30 years, but now both my brother and I have been struck down repeatedly by "tsetse naps." I switched to boxer shorts late last year, and this spring bought my first pair of "Bass" sandals. Hush Puppies are next.

I've also noticed new expressions creeping into my conversation. After flubbing a volleyball play: "25 years ago I would've had that!" On a date: "Mind if I drop you off early? I'm in the middle of a really good book right now." And the all-purpose: "That was before your time."

Yes, there now are people alive in the world who not only don't know about Woodstock and the wreck of the Andrea Doria, but who don't even care. They don't know who the Beatles were either, or Ozzie and Harriet — yet they claim to lead full, productive lives.

Many of these whippersnappers are old enough now to drive as fast as they can. They come glaring up from behind in a cloud of smoke and gravel, with fire in their bellies and enough flapping windsurf gear to rig a ghost ship. I always pull off the road and wave them by, knowing I'll coast up beside them at the first stop light.

Helen out at Larry's in Paia has noticed it, too. "Where are they all going in such a hurry?" she asked in exasperation. "Are they going to drive off Maui?"

"They're young yet," I said. "They think the island's not going to be here tomorrow."

Sunday afternoon at Hookipa, all ageism was off. There were two young windsurfers out in 20-foot surf, just a lime-green sail and a pink sail streaking across huge, terrifying waves. The whole ocean rolled and sucked and thundered, closing out the bay. Yet they jibed and sped out to sea again, showing incredible skill and courage.

And there was 83-year-old Eugenio LaCuesta, carrying his long pole and his afternoon's catch back to his car. "Five fish, 'nough," he smiled, lifting the lid of his creel. Stooped and frail, he had pulled his dinner from the same terrifying surf.

"What's your secret, at your age?" I asked.

"Eat plenty seaweed," he said.

— November, 1987

Single Maui Syndrome

As I knew he would, the roguish-looking man in the yellow silkie slid with practiced ease onto the bar stool that had opened on the other side of my date. He had well-formed muscles, a deep tan and an alligator grin.

"Pack your nose?" I heard him ask her softly.

"You're on," she replied. "Your place or mine?"

I tried to stammer an objection, but it got lost in the swirl of their departure.

"Nice talking with you," my date said over her shoulder. "Thanks for the drink."

And the dinner, I thought gloomily. And the pikake lei. And the dancing we didn't get to do.

I remembered the comforting words the minister had said in hippie church that Sunday: "You don't have to worry about what to say or what to do. You might not realize it right away, but there is a reason for everything that happens to you."

Somehow, the words didn't seem as comforting now as they had in church, but I knew they were true. There was a reason for this. I just didn't know what it was yet.

Swiveling slowly on my stool, I surveyed the room. It was hot, crowded and noisy, though not as smoky as it would have been five years earlier. The band was on an extended break — probably off packing their noses someplace — but they hardly seemed missed in the general roar of conversation. Except for a handful of strays at the bar, everyone seemed to know each other already, and they seemed deliriously happy to be there.

Drinks in hand, stylishly coiffed men in silkies and polo shirts circulated among the tables, confidence and charm radiating from their tan, smiling faces. Whether laughing with groups of pretty girls at the tables or speaking with burning intensity to the few women who remained at the bar, they seemed somehow ... invulnerable. They didn't have to worry about what to say or what to do, I realized. They had cocaine.

Or at least they looked like they had cocaine. Not all of them did, of course. Most of the ones who did have cocaine had already left, one or more of the prettiest girls on their arms. Bidding victorious farewells to their friends, they headed out the door toward some indescribably lascivious adventure I could only dimly imagine.

The band wandered back on stage, ran a sound check, then broke into a feverish rock anthem complete with thundering drums, wailing guitars and a gritty, floor-shaking bass. Eyes ablaze, long, fine legs glittering with sequins, the female vocalist lunged hungrily toward the crowd, mike in hand.

"Dontcha worry 'bout what to say, say, say or what to do!" she screamed. "Just pack my nose up tight, big stallion, and I'll spend the night with yooooouuu . . . ."

The dance floor filled rapidly with pulsing, bobbing bodies, but I didn't feel much like dancing. I scanned the tables out of long habit and saw that the unattached women had either left or become attached. I finished my drink and pushed a crumpled twenty toward the bartender.

"There's a reason for this," I told him thickly. "Everything happens for a reason."

He nodded briskly and, eyes averted, returned my change. "Drive home safely," he said.

Being a single male on Maui can be hard. Well, it's not easy anywhere else . . . but it seems especially hard here. Perhaps because Maui is an expensive, fashionable resort area devoted to one form of hedonism or another, it has more than its share of expensive, fashionable hedonists.

This can be discouraging to those of us who are not expensive, fashionable hedonists but who just live and work here. I mean, the beautiful ones are out there every day — jogging in the sunlight or pumping along on their bicycles, tanning themselves at poolside, windsurfing, playing backgammon or whatever they do.

I've got no grudge against them. They've earned their hedonism. It takes a lot of discipline and hard work to be hedonistic. You have to exercise vigorously, eat sensibly and tan evenly to be part of that scene. And you have to have money. Silkies and cocaine aren't cheap.

The problem is that the places where single people can go to meet each other — bars and nightclubs in Lahaina and Kihei, dance places at Wailea and Kaanapali — are basically oriented toward serving the beautiful ones. It's their playground, in effect, but we all have to play on it.

For men, it's a highly competitive playground — almost, at times, a proving ground. Are you built like Tom Selleck? Can you dance like Michael Jackson? Are your clothes thoroughly modern? How about gold neck chains — do you have enough of those? And how fat is your wallet — can it support dinner, several rounds of drinks, cover charge, tips, gas, grass and toot?

If you are a single male and you answer "no" to any of the above, you may be suffering from SMS — Single Maui Syndrome. This crippling disease turns normal, healthy, well-adjusted men into sterno drinkers.

The physical symptoms are easy to spot: a certain resigned sadness about the eyes, a tightness around the mouth caused by futile grinning, lips atrophied from disuse, and a body stiff from too much longing and too little tenderness. The psychological and emotional effects may be more damaging still. As the disease runs its course, the heart chakra ceases vibrating, the brain chakra falls into confusion and despair, and the libido chakra commits chakracide.

It's not a pretty sight. But the disease can be arrested if treated early enough. The latest scientific research indicates that the following measures may bring at least temporary relief:

— Get a dog, preferably a large, friendly one. These loyal, fun-loving mammals can give you at least some of the affection you need every day, and you won't have to pack their noses.

— Join a hippie church. You may not meet single women there, but at least the congregation is into heavy hugging before, during and after services. Scientists say the human male needs five hugs a day just for maintenance. Hippie church will take care of Sunday's quota.

— Avoid listening to AM radio, which only plays teenage love songs; and country radio, which only plays songs about broken hearts. Magazines featuring celebrity romances also should be avoided, as should TV commercials letting it be Lowenbrau.

— If your libido chakra is still flickering, quell it with heavy, regular exercise. Swim to Kauai. Push your car to work. Walk across Kaahumanu Avenue on your hands.

— Avoid nightclubs, singles bars and discos. Try your luck instead at "cultural" events like poetry readings, art gallery openings and plays. Many unescorted women go to these kinds of things. Unfortunately, the reason they're unescorted is because their husbands and boyfriends stayed home to play poker. But at least you can be in the same room with some interesting women.

— Better yet, go to a movie. Then you can boast to your friends that you were in a "big, dark room at night" with "many women" who "literally lined up" to be there with you.

— Sign up for a massage class. Lots of Maui women are into massage and health-related activities. You may get to work with one of them in the name of mind-body awareness. Probably, though, you will get paired off with another male.

— If you can get by without mind-body awareness, join an

aerobics dance class. These classes are 99 percent female. But don't try anything funny — most of these women are in far better shape than you are. By the time you've agonized through 90 minutes of leg kicks, butt-tighteners and tummy firmers, you'll understand why they only go out with stallions. But at least you'll be tired. Go home and read the funnies to your dog.

— Learn to cook . . . if not a wide variety of dishes, at least one show-stopper you can take to potlucks. Women are often impressed by men who can cook, and they might ask you for the recipe. When the meal is over, help clear the table and do the dishes instead of joining the other men for brandy and cigars in the library. Women tend to hang out in kitchens, and it is sometimes possible to engage them in conversation there. Ask them if they've read *Women Who Love Too Much*.

— Once in a great while, a woman may express interest in you. If this happens, tell her right off that you do not have cocaine. If she still seems interested, find out if she is married, has a steady boyfriend, or is fighting with one of the above. Jealousy is a potent force — even in this supposedly liberated age — and some women are not above flirting with lonely, unwitting dupes to make their partners or ex-partners jealous. Avoid these women at all costs . . . unless you want to spend the next six weeks taking your meals intravenously.

— Finally, if by some blind fluke of fate you meet an unattached woman who will sit and talk with you for five minutes without searching the room for studlier males, don't panic or run away. Breathe deeply. If your hands are trembling, keep them out of sight. Do not leer.

Instead, try to be calm, sincere and pleasant. Ask her about herself — her interests, hopes and misgivings — and solicit her views on subjects of current concern. Listen attentively and respectfully. Treat her as you would a cherished friend. It will probably be a novel, even amusing, experience for her.

Then, at the first opportunity, send her a bouquet of flowers. Some women still like flowers.

— June, 1983

43

Big Wind

Someone who wants to make money should stretch a big net between Maalaea and Kihei. The net would catch everything blown away in Central Maui — laundry, chicken coops, Cadillacs — and the owners could reclaim their property for a fee. Unclaimed goods could be sold at the swap meet.

I think it would work, because outside of the "Roaring 40s" belt around Antarctica, Central Maui may be the windiest place in the Pacific.

How windy is it? It's so windy here that birds call a cab, waves break backwards, toddlers have to carry rocks in their pockets, and you cross the street to water your own yard.

Sometimes Maui gets so windy you can hear conversations that started out someplace else. No lie. Why, just the other day I was across the street watering my yard when I heard voices.

"Eh, Edith, we go Runway 7," one voice said.

"Nah, I li' eat first," another replied. "We go okazu-ya."

I looked around, but there was nobody. There I was, standing in Maalaea, and the voices were coming from Kaahumanu Center! I kept listening. The wind was howling pretty well by then, so I could only make out partial conversations: ". . . and then I told him, if I ever see his car outside her house again" . . . . "$499.99 per month and no down payment!" . . . . "Go for two! Slide! Slide!" . . . . "Come on, Mom, all the kids have 'em."

Once I was driving past Ukumehame at dusk. As usual, the waves offshore were breaking backwards, but I didn't realize how windy it was until I saw an entire roof in the top of a kiawe tree. "Hmmm, windy night," I thought. Two seconds later the hood of my truck blew back and smashed my windshield. It was very exciting.

Those kinds of things are fairly unusual. It's the regular stuff that gets you in the end: untwisting the "laundry mummies" from the clothesline, searching for the runaway trash cans on garbage day. I feel especially sorry for the tourists. They come to Maui expecting some placid Garden of Eden — only to have half their possessions stripped away as they step off the plane.

44

And those little straw hat stores — how do they make it here? The only sensible headwear for Maui is the standard-issue ball cap. Cinched three notches too tight and screwed down over the forehead, it keeps the wearer's hair from blowing off.

In that connection, a study should be made to find out if Maui people lose their hair sooner than people in other places. Do our houses erode faster? Is our hearing affected by the constant buffeting of the wind?

WHAT?

I SAID: IS OUR HEARING AFFECTED BY THE ... never mind.

And how about contact lens wearers? Talk about suffering — they can't get ten steps out of the house before some wicked little dust devil has them stumbling for cover, screaming and clawing at their eyes.

I was up at a garage sale in Pukalani one day when one of those little cyclones popped out of nowhere, sucked up a wheelbarrow and spat it over a fence into the next yard. It just goes to show, you can't leave wheelbarrows lying around loose.

With those baby tornados, I don't know whether it's better to see them coming or not. Driving on the new highway behind Kihei, you can sometimes watch these whirling columns of dirt and trash blast across the mauka brushland:

"Criminy sakes, hon — look at that one! It must be 300 feet high!"

"It's ... it's heading this way, dear. What'll we do?"

"Don't worry — it's just air and twigs and stuff, and this here's a good ol' solid American Oldsmobile. It'll take a lot more than that little spinner to . . . ."

SSSSSHHHHHHHHRRRRRRRRRREEEEEEEEEEEEOOOOOOOO-OOOOO!!!!

Meteorologically speaking, Maui is a textbook example of the "Venturi effect" — the principle that a fluid speeds up when passing through a channel. Since wind could be called "fluid air," the principle applies when mountains block the wind's path.

On Maui we have a 6,000-foot mountain and a 10,000-foot mountain quite close together. Since the trade winds can't blow the mountains down, they take the path of least resistance — the low-lying "saddle" in between. Maalaea Bay is where all the wind in this part of the Pacific whooshes back out to sea after accelerating through the saddle.

I once worked as a cook for a tour boat company that had big plans to do deluxe "sunset dinner cruises" on Maalaea Bay: white linen tablecloths, candlelight, a roast beef dinner with all the trimmings. You name it.

I tried to warn those guys. But they had a 95-foot motor yacht with plenty of muscle, so they figured: "Hey, what's a little wind and chop? We'll plow right through it."

The ashtrays were the first to go. Light plastic jobs, they sailed off that boat like little frisbees and bobbed happily off into the sunset. There's probably an "ashtray beach" on Kahoolawe now. The white tablecloths were next. Most of those stayed on the boat, but they flapped so fiercely that the deck was soon awash in spilled food and drink.

The wind chop took care of whatever the wind didn't get. As the boat pitched and rolled, trays of glasses shot out of their overhead racks and shattered across the deck. Hot grease from the roast beef pans drooled onto the floor, and we galley workers learned to step lively.

I can still see the Hawaiian trio that tried to play music while the deck was yawing and heaving. The keyboard lady was a Trans-Pac veteran, so she was all right, but the guitarists had to cling to a beam with one hand and strum with the other. They did "Pearly Shells" a lot.

The tourists loved it — partly, I suspect, because the cruise featured unlimited mai-tais. The wind took their hats and visors immediately, and the chop sent many of them to the rails, but we never lost anyone overboard, so far as I know.

Nonetheless, the boat was sold to some San Francisco millionaire after a few months, and the tour company retreated to the flat, windless waters off Lahaina. I hear their ashtray bill has gone way down.

—April, 1984

The End of the World

The world is supposed to end again this week. The revelation of this most recent end of the world comes from numerologist Edgar Whisenant, author of *88 Reasons Why The Rapture Will Be in 1988*.

According to his calculations, the world will start to end at sunset today — about the time some of you normally lift the cat off the recliner and start reading this column.

Preoccupied with recent family sadness on Oahu, I didn't learn of Whisenant's revelation until I got back to Maui yesterday. I took the news dead seriously, as I always take the end of the world.

The last end of the world I lived through was in New York City in the summer of 1968. We were all supposed to leave Manhattan by some exact date — June 25th or 26th, I think. The city was going to slide into the Atlantic to start the end of the world. I read about it in the underground papers.

My fiancee and I stuffed our meager possessions into her old Volvo 544, said goodbye to stubborn New York friends, and sped westward across the darkening continent. We hoped to reach Illinois, where her family's home had a root cellar.

I checked the rear-view mirror as I drove, expecting the land behind us to fall suddenly away like a Hilo Creme dipped too long in cocoa. We also listened for telltale signs from the east — the grinding of tectonic plates, the roar of 400-foot tsunamis, or the fanfare of celestial trumpets.

Nothing. We tried the radio, but the Volvo's aged crystal set couldn't pull in New York. Instead, we got a staticky, mid-continental crossfire of AM night radio — The Shirelles warring with hog belly futures, zydeco from New Orleans, used cars in Omaha, cowboy songs from Calgary.

We reached Illinois without incident and staggered up to her parents' door sometime before dawn, road-weary and terminally buzzed on No-Doz.

"Why, what a surprise," her mom yawned, patting her curlers.

"Is it still there?" I asked.

"Whuun?" her father said. He had managed to sleepwalk down the stairs but was not yet ready for interlocution. His hair sprang from his head like coils from a burst couch.

"Is what still there, dear?" the Mrs. inquired.

"New York!" I said, my eyes jumping. "New York is gone!"

"We fled the city, Mom," my fiancee explained. "It was supposed to fall into the ocean during the night. We tried to hear the news on the radio but we could only get Hank Williams."

"Gone?" her dad grunted. "Shucks. The Cubs were supposed to play the Mets at Shea Stadium today. I'll have to wash the car."

The logic of this escaped me for the moment, but I had more pressing concerns. "May we stay in your root cellar for a few days?" I asked.

"Of course you may, dear," the Mrs. said in soothing tones. "Our root cellar is your root cellar. Have you had any breakfast? How about some nice Pop-tarts?"

"Pop-tarts!" I snapped. "How can I think of Pop-tarts at a time like this? The world may be ending even as we speak! New York may already be gone!"

In fact, even as we spoke, ominous red streaks appeared in the sky to the east. In the dark elms overhead, birds awoke and chirped in alarm.

"Suit yourself," my fiancee's mother said, scanning the new morning. "Just looks like another nice summer day to me. But if the world is ending, we might as well have breakfast."

Soon we were all in the kitchen eating Pop-tarts and scrambled eggs. There was no news of the New York disaster on radio or TV, but our host called Shea Stadium just to be sure. The ticket office was still closed, but he managed to reach one of the groundskeepers.

"Shea's still there," he told us, his hand over the mouthpiece. "He says the Cubs are taking batting practice now."

"But Shea's in Flushing Meadows!" I said. "That's not New York. Ask him if Manhattan's still there."

"He says the last time he looked it was — but he hasn't been there in years and doesn't care to go back."

I haven't been back, either, but I heard through the grapevine that New York is still there. Or it will be, at least until sunset today.

If it's after sunset and you're on your recliner reading this column, then the world's probably still here. If not, well — it's been grand. See you in the next one.

— September, 1988

Understanding Women

Today's column is for guys. Women turn the page, OK? Thanks.

Now, there has been talk that men and women still are not getting along. The problem is misunderstanding. We don't understand them, and they don't understand why. One reason is that, before today, no one has taken the time to just sit down and explain women's ways.

Women are not like other people. They are the only ones who bear and nurse children. They are emotionally, physically and spiritually equipped for this, just as we are equipped for greasing engines, felling trees and smoking cigars. A man is an island — especially when smoking a cigar — but a woman is a potential home.

This plays out in interesting ways. While a man may want a '64 Corvette or a seat on the 50-yard line, women tend to seek security, stability, tenderness, respect and understanding — the qualities that make for a good home.

Men seek these things, too, but we have been trained not to admit it — or much of anything, for that matter. We are especially good at not admitting our feelings. We are fluent in many languages — business, warfare, engineering, box scores — but the language of emotions was lost to us somewhere in childhood. It's easier just to talk about the game.

Women have many hardships in this life, but talking about their feelings isn't one of them. They go right to the heart of the matter, fearlessly and caringly. If their friend is sad, they say: "Are you feeling sad?" And the other one gushes out all her troubles. Then the first one gushes out all HER troubles, and they both go have a mineral water.

We don't do this, of course, because we're men. We say: "How's it goin'?" And the other guy says: "Great! How you been?" And the first one says: "Great!" Then we stride away manfully, our troubles intact.

While we're striding away, the women sip Calistoga and work through the big-ticket items: kids, schools, careers, Gorbachev, car trouble. That done, they plunge happily into "relationspeak," which

49

is their equivalent of our "sportspeak."

In relationspeak, the participants examine relationships — both theirs and other people's — down to the tiniest subatomic scintilla of hair-splitting nuance.

Where two or more women are gathered in relationspeak, let no man enter there. Ironically, one of the things they enjoy talking about most is men. Is he cute? Is he married? What was he wearing? Has he called? How much does he make?

Without men, women would be robbed of this inestimable pleasure, so in one sense they want relationships with us just as we want relationships with them. Only the motives are different. We want someone to go riding in the '64 Corvette. They want someone they can relationspeak about with their friends.

How does one strike up a relationship with a woman? In addition to being confident, stable, cheerful, prosperous, a great dancer and looking good in pastels, the man should not ask the woman what's for dinner. He also must give no sign that he wants a relationship.

This is the key, and the great Catch-22 for men seeking relationships with women: If you want one you can't have one because you want one. The corollary has an almost zen-like simplicity: If you seek happiness with a woman, be happy with yourself. Like much sage advice, this originally came from a monk.

Other tips: Women put great stock in appearances, so when meeting one for the first time, remember to shave and to wear a shirt or belt. If you wear shoes, socks are a good bet, and a nice Diner's Club card never goes out of style. In considering your appearance, though, don't overlook hers — in all likelihood, much time and expense has gone into its creation. Tell her she looks fabulous.

But what about her hair? How honest should you be? This is one area where we must take our cues from them. In all hair matters, women notice the subtlest changes and support each other maniacally. In fact, the first full sentence many girl babies exchange is: "I just wuv youw haiw!" Any new haircut or style, however startling, should be praised.

OK, women can turn the page back now.

Hi! Oh, we were just talking about the game. What's for dinner?

— January, 1988

Tom's Nasal Tours

I have a part-time job that takes me into "historic Lahaina Towne" once a week. On the way to the job, I pass many ingenious money-making ventures: gold by the inch, pry-your-own oysters with pearls inside, opportunities to adopt a whale.

Most impressive to me, though, are the rides and tours offered at the various activity kiosks. There seems to be something for everyone. You can coast down Haleakala on a bicycle or jounce down to Kalaupapa on a mule. You can trot around Maui on horseback, probe its coves in a Zodiac or buzz it by helicopter. You can watch whales from a boat or harrass them from a jet ski.

The tours are equally amazing. There are shopping tours and snorkel tours, restaurant tours and regional tours, social and religious and historical tours. There are even tours of artists' studios and bakers' kitchens.

"How can I get in on this bonanza?" I wondered, my nostrils flaring with avarice. Then it hit: No one has yet offered a nasal tour of Maui.

In addition to its more highly publicized features, Maui is a virtual spice cabinet of exotic scents, fragrances and odors. I'll bet tourists would pay through the nose to get a real insider's whiff of the island.

Because the concept is new, Tom's Nasal Tours would have to start small. I'd use my own car — itself a spice cabinet of exotic scents — and station one customer at each window. We'd probably go at night, since that's when the smells are strongest.

The $79.99 tour price would include a complimentary blindfold and a sachet of dried Maui flowers. This would be pressed to the nose between tour segments, much as a sherbet is used to "cleanse the palate" between courses of a fancy meal.

The complete nasal tour would include a West Maui loop — not only because that's where the richest tourists are, but because, mile for mile, that's the island's richest olfactory environment.

Starting at Kaanapali, we would whiff the sewage treatment plant, apply our sachets, then enjoy the hearty restaurant aromas of Front Street, followed by the sublime scent of plumerias at the

Puamana end of the street.

Back on the highway, the mouth - watering fragrances of teriyaki and barbecue would beckon from Launiupoko Park's grills, but then some rapid sachet work would be needed to get us past the burning tire smell at Olowalu Dump and the nearby "black death" smell of plantation waste water. Later we would slow for the rich, piquant aromas rising from Chez Paul before zooming through the sweet scent of kiawe blossoms along Ukumehame.

Our Central Maui leg would include a spin up Waiko Road, where the earthy odors of a feed lot, the old landfill site and a piggery give way at the mauka end to white ginger and wild guava. We would also feature a "restaurant row" segment, cruising past all the spicy Chinese, Japanese. Korean, Hawaiian and Italian eateries on Lower Main and Alamaha streets.

The pineapple cannery would be a must, as would a slow pass through Kahului itself, where some of America's most savory meals are prepared nightly. Then, passing the fried chicken smell at Kentucky Fried and the sizzling steak smoke of Naokee's, we would ascend into the cool, tropical nosescape of Iao Valley.

There we would smell yellow ginger and guava, rain and ironwood needles, red Maui mud and perhaps even the stream itself. A detour to Wailuku Heights would reward us with a fine whiff of eucalyptus.

For the best eucalyptus, though, we'd go Upcountry — past the cane-moist and pasture-dry smells, past piney cypress hedges and eye-watering poultry farms, past the chemical spray residues of flower farms and pineapple fields into the fog zone, where the eucalyptus smell is snappiest.

Other possible odoriferous zones for Tom's Nasal Tours include Maalaea mud flats (fishy), Paukukalo (ocean salty), Kahului Airport (aviation fuel-y) and the sharp, pure, icy air at the crater rim.

At the end of the tour, each customer would get a complimentary t-shirt with our motto: Maui Nose Ka Oi.

— February, 1988

Pop Ball

A recent encounter with Maui's newest fad toy, the "Pop Ball," has me gnashing my remaining teeth in admiration and dismay.

The admiration is for the product — a simple, cheap, pocket-sized toy certain to spread joy and laughter wherever it goes.

The dismay is because I didn't think of it.

You know the feeling? Just when it seems like everything useful or amusing in the whole world has already been invented, some clever bloke springs a new one on you.

Not that I could have invented the Pop Ball. It's a "scientific energy toy," and I got D plus in science. But I could have invented the surf leash, and I'm still kicking myself for that. I swam after my board for 15 years and never once thought of tying it to my ankle. Oh well.

For those who haven't seen one yet, the Pop Ball is a rubber hemisphere about the size of half a lemon. It has no visible moving parts, but it can rocket into the air simply by being inverted and placed or dropped onto a flat surface.

Longs has been selling 150 of them a week since mid-September, but I didn't see one until a news assignment took me to Baldwin High School the other day.

Two guys were standing face-to-face in the hallway after school. At first I thought they were going to beef, but they were smiling. As I approached, there was a sharp "pop" on the ground at their feet, and a little blue disc shot up between them like a champagne cork.

Both guys had lightning reflexes, and one of them managed to snag the thing in mid-flight while the other snatched air. The victor placed the disc on the ground again, and the two waited, crouched and laughing, for the next pop.

"Rad!" I thought. For something so small and simple, Pop Ball delivers more fun than most of the $2.99 items I've seen in my pleasure-seeking life. It has all sorts of spunky attributes: flight, speed, sound, surprise, portability, durability . . . .

Versatility is probably in there, too. Like Frisbee, it looks like the kind of toy you could invent whole new sports around. And, like Hackysack, it can be enjoyed alone, by two players or in a group.

There's also just enough nuisance value to put Pop Ball into novelty stores alongside such hoary rib-ticklers as the handshake buzzer, Whoopee Cushion, squirting lapel flower and "black eye" kaleidoscope.

I haven't worked all this out yet, but it seems to me that something small enough to be concealed in one's hand — and something which rockets into the air a few moments after placement — could stir up all kinds of mischief in a variety of settings.

Say your friend is about to start in on a big order of pancakes at IHOP. You wait until he's spread the butter and has the blueberry syrup jug poised.

"Wo — check that tarantula!" You point, he whirls around, you slip the Pop Ball beneath the top cake, he turns back.

"Where?" he asks suspiciously.

"It ran away."

He tilts the syrup jug and starts forming the sweet, sticky spiral characteristic of pancake eaters. Then — "pop!" — a rubber disc rips through the pancake, spraying your amazed friend with syrup and warm pulp.

No? OK, how about in the operating room. Your co-surgeon has made the major incision, exposing the duodenum and the thoracic cavity. She turns to the vital signs monitor. You slip a sterilized Pop Ball beneath the pancreas and stand back, grinning expectantly behind your mask.

Too unprofessional? All right. Let's say you're in the lingerie department at Liberty House. . . .

On second thought, Liberty House is a major advertiser here at *The Maui News.* Maybe we should just stick to placing the Pop Ball safely on a level surface near home or school and leave it at that.

I'm sorry to go on about such a seemingly trivial subject, but let me just say this.

We journalists spend entire careers trying to make the world a teensy bit better place. Then something comes along that actually does make the world a better place.

What can you do but salute?

— October, 1988

Driving on Maui

I was a kid when I first heard about hell. Mean Stanley next door told me about it. He said it was a hot place underground where devils poked you with pitchforks and where shave ice melted before you could eat it. He said I was sure to end up there.

I took my younger brother out to the back yard and made him dig a hole with my shovel. He went as deep as he could, but he didn't find any devils — just worms and rocks. And the ground was cool, not hot. I told Mean Stanley that there wasn't any hell after all, laughed at him, and rode my bike to the store for a shave ice.

Now, 30 years later, I realize than Mean Stanley was at least partly right: there is a hell, but it's not underground. Hell is trying to make a left turn in Lahaina.

There's really nothing like it. The broiling sun turns your car into a crematorium while the endless Lahaina Train rolls by in front of you. Not the "sugar cane train" — I'm talking about the train of vehicles on Honoapiilani Highway stretching as far as the eye can see in both directions, vehicles filled with tourists who don't know where they're going.

There's an Upcountry Train, too. It inches down Haleakala Highway at 7:00 in the morning and crawls back up at 4:30 in the afternoon. The people in that train at least know where they're going, but it doesn't seem to help.

The lead car in the Upcountry Train always goes 32 miles an hour — even downhill — and the 977 cars behind it all have to go 32 miles an hour, too. If you pull out to pass, you run into the train coming the other way. Then you get to test your suspension in the potholes along the shoulder, some of which are deep enough to have devils inside.

Once the morning Upcountry Train reaches Kahului, the commuters get to run the red lights on Kaahumanu Avenue. Now, some people may tell you that the lights on Kaahumanu Avenue aren't synchronized, but they are. If you go 47 miles an hour you can make the first two; then slow to 8 miles an hour for the Beach Road intersection; then accelerate to 156 miles an hour going past

Kaahumanu Center and MCC. Nothing to it.

Wailuku is a different story. No matter what speed you travel, what direction you're going, or what time of day you enter the town, you'll never make both lights on Main Street. Going downhill, you always get stuck behind someone who doesn't know yet that the red light with the green arrow under it means "keep going." Traveling uphill, you always hit the red light at Market Street. Many clutches have gone to hell on that hill.

Other interesting features of Maui's roadways include the Kihei Road Slalom, where daring drivers test their reflexes by weaving through an obstacle course of manhole covers that tower a foot or more above the surrounding pavement. These bothersome humps can become helpful markers, though, when heavy rains submerge the road between Greater Suda Lake and Azeka Slough.

Heavy rains also offer automotive challenges on Baldwin Avenue, where drivers traveling mauka during a storm are apt to confront miniature flashfloods sweeping logs, rocks and pit bulls downhill.

While these situations are temporary, there are some elements of driving on Maui that are as eternal as the "hit the brakes no-signal right turn" and the "stop in the middle of the road to talk to your friend." These customs, like the empty six-pack jettison, are cherished Maui driving traditions that predate tourism and synchronized stoplights.

In those days, driving on Maui was a fairly simple process. Everybody drove World War Two army jeeps, and there weren't that many places to go. Basically, you just drove through the cane fields, firing your rifle at road signs, then turned around and drove back. At night you could drive to Tasty Crust.

Then came the Sheraton-Maui, an early increment of what was to become the Kaanapali resort area. People started driving out there to see this new wonder, and soon the first Lahaina Train was snaking around the pali. On New Year's Eve, every operable car and jeep on the island could be found slowly circling the new resort, its horn honking.

Big-time tourism brought fast new roads to Maui and slow old tourists to drive on them. Maps spread open in their laps, gray heads swiveling, they would creep along the roads like tortoises, trying to make sense of street signs that all seemed to read: "Kuihehikilanihonoapiimehamehaiki."

Tour buses also joined the island's driving mix at about that time, but only those with broken mufflers and leaky exhaust systems were allowed on the road — a tradition that still holds to this day.

The condo boom that followed Kaanapali added hundreds of huge construction rigs to island roadways, all moving as fast as possible to haul as much stuff as possible so everybody could make as much money as possible to buy sleeker, faster cars for the New

Year's Eve drive to Kaanapali.

These heavy construction rigs pounded Maui's old two-lane roads to mochi, and soon every road with a quarry at one end and a condo project at the other was cratered with potholes. The whole island was like a war zone, with drivers zig-zagging around bomb craters and dodging bouncing cinderblocks while gravel from speeding, overloaded trucks crackled off the windshield like machine gun fire.

Once the condominiums were all built, people came to Maui to stay in them. Some of these people were young and foolhardy enough to fill their heads with dope and wobble along the roadsides on rented "mopeds." These motorized toys have a top speed of 25 miles an hour, making them excellent targets for the 40-knot crosswinds that sweep down from Ukumehame.

Along with the young moped riders came "part-time" residents who would spend just enough time in their Mainland or Canadian hometowns each year to forget where their Maui "second home" was. Soon these confused new part-Mauians proudly took their places at the head of the Lahaina and Upcountry Trains, traveling just fast enough to create the illusion of movement.

I was sitting in my blue '71 Crematorium at the Pizza Hut intersection in Lahaina one recent afternoon, growing old and crazy waiting to make a left turn, when one of these endless trains went by. A part-Mauian flanked by mopeds was in the lead, followed by gravel-spraying construction trucks, map-reading visitors, smoking tour buses, *Grapes of Wrath* hippie trucks, pakalolo - scented surfmobiles and beer bottle - ejecting four - wheelers.

Finally the last car approached, and I thought I glimpsed a familiar face behind the wheel — one I hadn't seen in 30 years. Sure enough, it was Mean Stanley.

He slowed down just long enough to laugh at me.

— September, 1982

Shoes

Artful Dodger manager Nancy Coombs called the other day to say that her feet had won $75 and a trip to Oahu.

Apparently the Redwing Shoe people held a statewide talent search for "Hawaii's biggest feet." Nancy entered a tracing of her size 12s and took second place in the women's division. She and the other Neighbor Island winners were to be flown to Honolulu to have their footprints immortalized in cement at the Redwing store.

I was bitterly disappointed that no one told me about the contest. If a mere size 12 was worth $75 and a trip to Oahu, I calculated, my feet could have won a Mercedes and a trip to Massachusetts, where the first shoe factory was built in 1760.

We go now to Colonial Massachusetts, where two guys with buckles on their shoes talketh story:

"Well met, Ephraim — what sayest thou, dude? Thy shoe factory is completed, I see. Prithee, how wilst thou makest thy shoes?"

"We shall maketh them tiny and narrow, Eli, so as to save leather. The Revolution loometh. We shall need our leather for saddles and funny-shaped hats."

"Aye, but what shape wilst thou givest thy shoes?"

"I shall shape them like Italy. I have always fancied that high arch and prettily pointed toe."

" 'Tis indeed a shapely land, Eph — but no fit model for a shoe, methinkest. What sayest thou to using the human foot itself as a model?"

"Ho, ho! Thou jokest, Eli! No shoe on God's good earth hast ever resembled a human foot. Nay, our task is to make the foot resemble the shoe!"

Ever since then, shoe factories have marched out millions of narrow, pointy little shoes, and we have had to force our feet into them, grunting like Cinderella's stepsisters. (The stepsisters weren't really wicked, by the way — their feet just hurt. Cinderella, who went barefoot, was relentlessly cheerful.)

The tragic consequences are everywhere: toes piled up like a train derailment, the nails ingrown, the foot itself hideously deformed by bunions. It saddens me to look at a baby's feet — so wide and wiggly-toed — knowing that some day that baby will hobble as an adult toward the Dr. Scholl display in Longs, just another victim of crippling shoe impairment. You think babies don't know? That's why they cry.

I think everybody would be happier if the first shoe factory had started here in the islands, where feet have a long and respected heritage. In hula, in lomilomi, in bodysurfing and in retrieving volleyballs from coconut trees, there is no substitute for the wide, powerful, toe-gripping "luau foot."

If the first shoes had been made in Hawaii, they would have been much more humane than the pinchy little ones we have now. They might even be shaped like Maui — with Haleakala as the main foot part, nice and roomy, and Puu Kukui as the heel. Molokai's shape would make a snappy-looking penny loafer.

Even though island people have to wear shoes more often than they used to, they're still way luckier than Mainlanders. Because of snakes, Mainland people have to wear shoes shaped like Italy from birth until death — even in the house. It's very sad.

As a result, their feet get knobbier and twistier and more painful until they either die or move away from snakes. A lot of them move here. The usual reasoning is that they come here for the weather, but I think it's so they can hobble around the house barefoot.

Bad as it is for Mainlanders, it's way worse for fashionable women. With the possible exception of the bound "Lily Foot" of Imperial China, I can imagine no fate crueler than to stalk about on high heels with my toes gravity-packed into a tight triangle the size of a cheese wedge. No wonder the women in those New York fashion ads always look so angry.

Nancy Coombs grew up in New York ("I had blisters all my life"), but she's not angry now. She moved two years ago to Hawaii, where feet are respected — and where big feet can even win prizes.

— March, 1988

100-Year Storm

Enough already with this weather!

Every day it's the same thing: droopy gray skies leaking rain. Sometimes a drizzle, sometimes a downpour, but never a rainbow. Seems like it's been going on for months — long enough to turn shower stalls into centipede condos and softball gloves into sprout farms. Little by little, people are going crazy.

I went into an auto glass shop in Wailuku to have my smashed windshield replaced.

"Did a rock bounce into it?" the man asked, surveying the ugly spiderweb of cracks.

"No," I said sheepishly. "I did it myself, with my hand. I was angry about something."

"Don't feel too bad," the man said. "There've been a lot of those kind lately. Must be the weather."

"Must be the weather" has become a popular refrain on Maui as residents try to explain the abrupt mood shifts that have characterized Valley Isle life since the last time anyone here saw a tan line, a bikini or a shadow.

It's not a pretty sight — a whole island going cuckoo for want of sunshine and color. I mean, this used to be a pretty colorful place. Lush green hillsides. Smoldering purple sunsets. Sparkling blue oceans. Now it's as monochromatic as a Pennsylvania foundry town in winter. The only thing missing is blackened slush in the gutters.

As the soundtrack for this endless, dismal movie we have the Maui Bronchial Chorus. Hacking coughs punctuate every attempt at conversation, and woe be to he who laughs, for laughter leads to rattling explosions of phlegm, followed by sputtering, choking and loss of breath. Stand by with the Heimlich Maneuver.

Next, consider the pervasive smell of mildew. On bath towels that won't dry. On belts and shoes that turn green. On the seats of Baldwin Auditorium. On the pieces of fruit you arranged so artfully in a bowl.

And how about the desperate scene at the laundromat? Scores of men and women lugging huge baskets of mildewed, mud-spattered clothing from W&F to Wash House and back again in a relentless search for a dryer that doesn't have a phalanx of steely-eyed housewives camped in front of it.

Well, at least the laundromats are profiting from all this. And the bars. They've never had it so good. All these tourists and residents, denied their normal round of healthful, outdoor activity, seek solace in drink and conversation.

But what's the conversation about? The Weather. Nobody's talking about gardening or windsurfing or politics . . . or even real estate. Nope. They're saying: Can you BELIEVE this?

"We've been here three whole weeks," some tourist matron will say, twirling the little umbrella from her mai-tai, "and it hasn't let up for a minute, not a minute. The first few days I told my Elmer, well, this is a blessed relief from Saskatoon, eh? But the second week was just as bad, you know, and we finally decided we'd fly over to Laniay or Molykaiya and see if it was any better over there, but of course it wasn't and now we have to go back home tomorrow as pale as ghosts and no one will believe we were even here, eh?"

"I've been living here 10 years," some silkied swiftie in neck chains and coke spoons will say, "and I've never seen it like this."

"I been here all my life, brah," a local guy will conclude. "Dis is notting."

Among the hardest hit are those shrewd North Americans who bought Maui property during the booming 1970s, when everything that wasn't bolted down was for sale, and when the sun seemed like it would shine forever.

What the buyers didn't know then was that Maui was in the midst of a drought that would last a decade. Hell, people were falling all over each other to buy land in "sunny Nahiku" and "sun-drenched Kaupakalua;" could hardly wait to gaze up into the "blue skies of Olinda" from the decks of their pole houses.

The first indication that things were returning to normal was the "hundred year storm" of January, 1980 — now known simply as the "1980 Storm." What we didn't realize at the time was that that episode — with its floods, falling trees, and miles of muck — was only the start of the "hundred year storm."

We're in the second year of it now.

— March, 1982

Think Too Much

It's "Column McNugget" time again, time to free-associate on random, useless trivia out of sheer laziness.

Actually, I shouldn't demean this process. Thinking about trivia is grueling work. For instance, just the other day I was thinking. I was walking along Kaahumanu Avenue, under bombardment from the usual random thoughts that strike trivia columnists, when I passed Central 76, where my green Rolls was being serviced.

I call my car the green Rolls because it still rolls, thanks to Central 76. As I walked past it, I noticed how forlorn it looked there on the lot: driverless, rusty, facing the wrong way.

Immediately, I was attacked by thoughts. If a cactus falls in the desert, does it make a sound? If I'm not in my car, do I still exist? Why does the car only seem forlorn when I'm not in it?

I bumped into my old friend Elaine at Idini's. I hadn't seen her in years, since she moved to the jungle to get away from people like me. She was forthright as always. "Hi, Tom. Long time no see. Gee, you look terrible."

"I've been thinking."

"I'm sorry to hear that," she said. "Anything worthwhile?"

"No, just the usual. Whether I exist away from my car, why babies eat sand, is the green flash really green. You know."

"Why?"

"Why what?"

"Why do it?"

"Somebody's got to do it," I said, drawing myself up. "Those random, meaningless thoughts are always out there, buzzing around like flies, waiting to land on somebody. I just seem to attract them. I'm like flypaper for stupid ideas."

"They can't all be stupid," she said helpfully.

"Well, I did have one good one the other night," I said, brightening a little. "You know how the airlines and the phone companies deregulated? Well, I was wondering what would happen if the utilities deregulated."

She nodded, waiting.

"I mean, you could have any damn thing. 'Al's Nuclear Power.' 'Murakami Water Supply.' 'Wanda's Biomass Conversion — We Burn While-U-Wait.'"

"Now that's a stupid idea," she said. "Don't use that one."

****

OK. Instead we have this classified ad from *The Maui News* of April 6, referred by my esteemed colleague Harry Eagar, no mean trivialist himself:

"Wash dishes for the rich and famous at Kapalua Bar and Grill," the ad said. It was a funny ad, but because I think too much, I didn't realize it was funny.

At first I thought it was needlessly arrogant. I mean, dirty dishes are dirty dishes, right? And it's not like the dishwasher gets to come out of his steamy, fly-blown work station to meet Linda Evans because she liked the shallots in wine sauce.

But then I remembered my own days as a dishwasher to the rich and famous, and I relented. In 1967, I washed their dishes at a coy little French country inn near the Pownal, Vermont race track — a place that attracted rich and famous people the way I attract stupid ideas.

The good thing about the rich and famous — besides the fact that they stay out of the kitchen — is that they don't eat their food. The better and costlier the entree, the less they eat of it. This is one way the rich and famous show their power.

(Actually, they probably don't like shallots in wine sauce any more than the rest of us, but they're too polite to say so. They just go back to their yachts and have a bowl of Fritos.)

Anyway, because the rich and famous barely glanced at their meals, my dog and I ate tres, tres well that autumn: Chateaubriand for two.

****

Now this:

I opened my paper the other day and out fell this little booklet from Sears, all about the Sears Days Preview Sale. Flipping through it, I realized rather sadly that I didn't want or need anything in it — and there were hundreds of useful, fabulous, quality items in there.

After 40 years of wanting something, this realization was a change in life for me — like the first time I looked in the mirror and saw through my hair. I was pretty sad until I turned to page 50 and saw my favorite price — $999.99 — for something called a "camcorder." I barked with laughter.

Youngblood swiveled around. "Don't laugh," he said. "It works — your brain sees all those 9s, so we think it costs $900."

"Ron," I said. "You think too much."

—April, 1988

Podmo's Great Adventure

Once upon a time, in a galaxy far, far away, lived Podmo the Small. Podmo was the youngest in a family of salt miners who toiled under the five suns that beat down on the red dust planet Xandar.

Xandar had not always been a dust planet, and Podmo's people had not always been salt miners. Once, before The War, their world had been blue and green, an ocean planet dotted with islands.

In those times, the gentle Xandas were expert fishing people, lovers and singers, but only mediocre comedians. They told long, complex jokes that would seem quite boring to us, and they forgot some punch lines. They also amused each other with table magic, though their webbed paws made successful card tricks a rarity.

Like his parents and his 10 brothers and sisters, Podmo was round and furry, with bright golden eyes, a stub tail and a warm nose. With their stout limbs and webbed swimming paws, the Xandas looked like huge, seagoing teddy bears — all except Podmo, who looked like a small, seagoing teddy bear.

Before The War, when such things still mattered, Podmo's parents worried about his small size. Even at the age of six monsoons, when most Xanda cubs can start wearing their elders' goggles and fins, little Podmo was still no bigger than a jellyfish jar.

This was handy for Podmo, who loved jellyfish more than any other food, but it troubled his father, Big Daddymo, and his mother, Lady Dimo.

"I'm afraid our little cub will never grow to full size," Big Daddymo said one day when Podmo was out making sand cottages on the beach. "He'll never be big enough to take his place at the nets."

"It's so sad," agreed Lady Dimo, wringing her paws. "He's the sweetest one, too. How will he ever find a girlfriend?"

Podmo's brothers and sisters and their friends were well aware of the situation, but they never teased him about it, first because they loved him, and second because Xandas didn't make fun of others. Instead, they put Podmo in charge of the smallest fish in the catch, and he did his job proudly.

Podmo was herding minnows in the family's holding pond when The War came to Xandar. The first sign was the darkening of the sky — a thing that had never happened before, since the planet's five suns provided continuous, overlapping daylight.

Because of the overlapping daylight, the Xandas had never seen night or the stars, and so did not realize that there might be other beings out there besides Xandas and fish — beings with no sense of humor at all.

The Slitherians!

The Slitherians lived only for war and salt. Cunning, evil reptoids, their armored scales and rows of razor teeth struck terror into life forms throughout the known galaxy. Their great war fleets darkened the skies of many a planet, but only the blue and green ocean worlds felt the full lash of their tyranny.

When the Slitherian starfleet massed over Xandar, darkening the islands and the sea, the Xandas for the first time felt fear ice their hearts. As was their custom when greeting relatives or strangers, though, they stood in family groups, lifted their open paws skyward and sang their ancestral songs of welcome.

"This is going to be easier than we thought," the Slitherian commander hissed to his generals, his whip-like tongue flicking obscenely. "Gum them!"

With that, a blizzard of whirling, gummed nets descended on the Xandas from the hovering starships, snaring most of the population within minutes. Caught by surprise, they struggled mightily, but their exertions only tightened the sticky bonds. Having known only peace, the few Xandas who avoided capture and tried to defend themselves with stones and branches were no more than target practice for the heavily armed Slitherian storm troopers.

The War, such as it was, lasted only half a monsoon — a disappointingly short conquest for the murderous Slitherians, some of whom were soon sporting Xanda fur boots and hats. Finally all the Xandas had been captured and enslaved — all but Podmo, who was small enough to slip through the eyes of the net and hide in a jellyfish jar.

There he watched in horror as the salt-mad Slitherians turned their nuclear laser cannons on Xanda's shallow blue ocean and vaporized it, leaving only a red dust world crusted with salt. In short order, the heavily guarded Xandas were put to work mining salt for export to the far reaches of the Slitherian Empire.

Xandar was a rich find, but the insatiable Slitherians soon lusted for still more salt. They readied a drone probe to explore another blue and green planet rumored to lie third from the sun in a remote corner of a distant galaxy known to them only as The Salty Way.

This probe mission was classified top secret, but arrogant

Slitherian intelligence officers seeking to impress each other at cocktail parties let slip a few key details. These were picked up by the sharp-eared Xanda serving girls and relayed to Big Daddymo in his cell.

"You must somehow get aboard that probe and go for help," he told Podmo, who had entered the slave barracks hidden in a swordfish pie. "You are the smallest one, but our biggest hope. Peace go with you."

"Be brave and smart, my cub," Lady Dimo whispered from the next cell. "We will not see you again, but you will always be with us. Take this pendant and wear it for me." She pressed her only treasure, a small black pearl on a thin chain of gold, into his paw.

At length the probe ship stood ready on its firing pad, but before the gantries were rolled away, Xanda slave laborers had been able to hide little Podmo in the barrel of blue ink that fed the probe's salinity readout teleprinters. Tiny goggles protected his eyes, and a hidden breathing tube had been punched into the barrel for him.

Traveling at the speed of light squared, the probe rocket left Xanda's gravitational field and soon streaked beyond the five suns. Popping open the ink barrel, Podmo clambered into the probe's tiny cabin and went to the camera viewports, leaving webbed blue pawprints on the deck.

First he saw his own reflection. "I am blue now," he thought sadly. But his dismay at his new color vanished the moment he looked through the window. There, for the first time, he saw the stars.

They blazed like precious gems in the black velvet jewel box of space — huge red ones and tiny blue ones, white ones flashing like diamonds, yellow and orange and green ones. Spiral galaxies shimmered and pulsed with nets of silken light, and crab nebulae throbbed with distant, fiery majesty.

Pressing his nose to the viewport, Podmo gazed in rapture at the glory of the heavens, losing any sense of the passage of time or distance. Finally the probe's rockets fell silent, their fuel spent, and Podmo found himself in orbit above a blue and green planet that circled a small yellow sun.

Also orbiting the planet was a single moon, as gray and monotonous and barren as its larger companion was colorful and cloud-moist.

The remote-control surveillance unit whirred to life on a signal from the Slitherian commander half a universe away ... but the Slitherians had not foreseen a small blue stowaway. Grasping the controls carefully, Podmo aimed the camera and its battery of sensors at the airless, cratered surface of the barren moon.

Seconds later, the cockpit telefaxer began sending photo images back through space, and electronic impulses beeped the following readout in Slitherian: "Oxygen, negative. Water, negative. Edible salts, negative. No enslavable life forms. Contact planet of no apparent value. Recommend terminate probe. Repeat, terminate probe."

"Slime!" cursed the Slitherian commander, gnashing his fangs and driving a spiked jackboot through the telefax unit. "That planet's not worth its salt!" To his adjutant he roared: "Captain, bring me the head of whoever squandered our probe on this worthless world! Water planet, indeed!"

Jerking angrily back to his console, the commander punched a red key labeled "Arm Probe Termination Device," and the red key began to flash ominously. The words "Termination Device Armed" appeared moments later on the console screen.

The commander then stabbed a second red key marked "Detonate," his fury at losing his only deep-space probe ship leavened slightly by the pleasure of blowing something up.

Though the command zipped toward the probe's nuclear termination device at the speed of light squared, it was an elephant in molasses compared to the bright winged being who now appeared before the dazzled Podmo in the probe's tiny cabin. He had never seen a being so beautiful . . . or one his own size.

"Come with me, Podmo," she smiled, taking his paw in her little warm hand. "We've got places to go and people to see. This is a very special night, and it couldn't happen without you."

"But I can't go with you," he said, dabbing his sudden, hot tears with a webbed paw. "I'm a swimmer, not a flyer. And I can't breathe out there."

"You can do anything," she said. "Just believe, and it will be so."

"You're an angel," he said.

"Yes, I am," she smiled. "Here we go!"

With that, Podmo and the little angel streaked earthward hand in paw, while the sky behind them lit up like a white-hot magnesium flare as the probe ship's nuclear device detonated. The intense, fiery light would hang in that part of the heavens for days.

In the desert darkness far below, three wise but travel-weary kings looked up as a new star lit the Levantine winter sky. "There it is, as foretold!" said Balthazar. "Let us follow its beacon."

And in fields where shepherds lay with their flocks, and in towns where humble, beaten people ached for peace, where orphaned children ached for love, an angel rushed through the night, bringing tidings of comfort and great joy.

The chronicles of that great night do not include Podmo, though some who saw claimed that a blue garment trailed the Christmas angel on her rounds. And not one of the thousands of artists who painted the nativity scene through the centuries included a small, blue, bear-like being among the animals gathered that night in a Bethlehem stable.

Nor does any account of the birth scene record among the treasures left at the foot of the manger a small black pearl on a thin chain of gold.

No, these things — like the source of the sudden star that lit that night — are only the musings of an odd, story-telling Earthman 20 centuries later, a dubious amusement for a Christmas Day.

But the chronicles of Xanda shed some light. It is written there that Podmo the Small, later renamed Podmo the Peace Bringer, rode a rocket to another world, saw the stars, met an angel his own size and discovered that he could do anything he wanted, if he just believed.

Coincidentally, it is also recorded that shortly after Podmo's great journey, the heavens above Xanda opened, and torrential rain fell for 40 days and 40 nights, refilling the dry sea beds and forever driving off the wicked Slitherians, who knew a Greater Force when they saw one.

The Xandas took to the flood like the seagoing teddy bears they are, and soon were fishing and loving and singing as expertly as ever. All this makes the chronicles a pleasant read, but there is one sour note. A single clause in the chronicles reports that the Xandas are still mediocre comedians, and they proved it by calling that one the Xanda Clause.

Whew. Merry Christmas.

— December, 1987

Molokai Boys' Salute, Kaunakakai. Published July 7, 1976.

Hula dancer, Kaunakakai. Published May 2, 1976.

Young paniolo, Hana Ranch rodeo. Published Nov. 29, 1976.

Andy Bumatai and fans, Maui Zoofest. Published April 12, 1982.

Maui political candidates. Published Aug. 22, 1974.

Sand-eater and mom, Kihei. Published Dec. 12, 1983.

ESSAYS

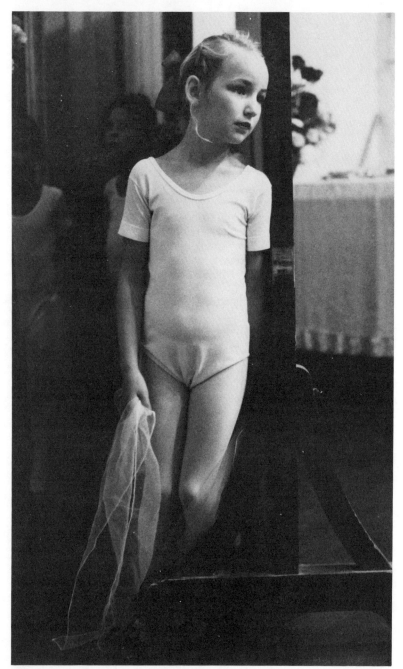

Makawao ballet student before recital. Published June 2, 1983.

Ballerinas

Toe shoes and tutus do not a Dame Margot make, but something special happens when little girls slip those ribboned satin shoes onto their feet, tie the gauzy skirts around their waists and become . . . ballerinas.

Little boys, all "snips and snails and puppy dog tails," can never quite figure it out — even when they become fathers of ballerinas. But to little girls and little girls grown, there is no doubt at all.

To be a ballerina, even for a night, is to dance in a dream.

As recital night nears, a wondrous transformation occurs. Spirited island girls who climb trees and throw rocks at their brothers, girls with freckles on their faces and bandaids on their knees, turn into butterflies.

Cheeks glowing with unaccustomed rouge, sparkling eyes highlighted with liner and brow pencil, they wait off-stage for the grownups to stop talking, for the house lights to dim, for the shining moment to arrive.

The weeks of rehearsal are over. The warmup stretches, the plies at the barre, the teacher's endless "repetez, repetez." After patient tutoring and considerable exertion, 8 - year - old awkwardness has become 8-year-old grace.

Now, as they wait for the phonograph needle to drop into the grooves of "Swan Lake" or "Peter and the Wolf," expectation shining in their eyes, they seem like faeries from some gentler, bubble world.

They are, right now, in magic. This is what it is for. The afternoons of practice, the parents' many car pools from school to studio to home — all lead to this fragile moment.

It is not the performance, really. That will go as well as it should — a festival of bright costumes and swirling motion ending in a proud thunder of applause.

There will be refreshments afterwards, and many pictures taken. Praise will rain on the teacher and her pupils. The parents will be pleased that they helped create something special for their daughters.

But the dance is not timeless as the wistful fantasy of the

waiting dancer. That cannot be photographed, or caught and held in the heart.

The grownups know this, especially the mothers. The beauty of this expectant moment stirs something deep in them, and they ache. Time is passing. Youth, which stretches ahead infinitely for the ballerinas, is so very short, and innocence so innocent.

There is a moment in nature — in the still, cool hour just before sunrise — when the very earth seems to hold its breath. The birds sleep. The light wind dies. A crystalline hush settles over all.

The waiting ballerinas are like that, in a way. No longer keikis, not yet women, they toe-balance between dream and wakefulness. To them the stage is not a stage. The crowded auditorium is not a darkened room.

The ballerinas are not there.

They are, right now, in magic.

— June, 1983

Candy

It was one of those late hours when friends tire of arguing about the pressing issues of the day and turn their eyes and thoughts to the heavens.

This was not hard to do on that particular night, since the people were already lying on their backs on the kicked-up turf of an outdoor volleyball court. Overhead, the soft Hawaiian sky was creamy with stars.

No one spoke for a long time, except to mark the occasional passage of meteors. Finally, someone pointed out the Milky Way.

"Milky Way?" another said. "I used to eat those."

With that, the conversation turned to the subject of "hana buttah days" — and candy.

As the constellations danced their eternal hula overhead, an entire galaxy of candies passed in memory's review: Milky Ways and Mars bars, Sugar Babies and Chocolate Babies, Sen-Sen and si moi, Lifesavers and Necco wafers, licorice whips and candy cigarettes with red "lit" tips.

Jujy Fruits and Jujubes, juice sticks and jawbreakers; butterscotch, bubble gum, Butterfingers and butter rum; spearmint, Beamon's and Black Jack gum; Good and Plenty, Junior Mints, bon-bons and Pom-Poms; Tootsie Rolls, Tootsie Pops, Heath bars, Hershey bars, Look bars, Big Hunk bars . . . .

Many of these sweets are still around today, but others have passed on to that great candy counter in the sky, along with colored popcorn and kiddie matinees.

It was at these Saturday afternoon children's movies that some of the most memorable candies were to be found. And "found" is the word, because the jostling, tight-packed crowd at the lighted candy counter left little room for viewing the sugary display.

Kids accompanied by tall people — like adults or eighth graders — could get visual reports from on high, but the adults often had a peculiar blind spot for the really good stuff. Instead, they would hand down things like pistachios or corn nuts.

The kids who really lived it up were the ones who got dropped off by their friends' mothers or who rode the bus to the theater with their neighborhood gang. They didn't have to worry about adults for a whole afternoon. They were entering Candy Heaven.

Then as now, different people liked different things. Bullies liked juice sticks, because the wax tubes that remained after the juice was gone could be used as blowguns, with the wax chewed up bit by bit for ammo. Some girls liked Violets and could be located in those darkened theaters by the sweet, pungent smell that candy gave off.

Lik-M-Ade junkies could be recognized by their purple (or green or red) index fingers, and kids who liked little tin toys could be seen clutching boxes of Tomoe-Ame. These contained, in addition to the "prize," small cubes of gelatinous candy in rice paper wrappers that dissolved on the tongue.

Kids who liked to pace themselves often chose candies which made up in number what they lacked in bulk: M&Ms, lemon drops, candy hearts, Lifesavers, malted milk balls and the like. With these, it was possible at any point to figure out how many were left, how slowly they should be eaten, and whether they should be crunched up quickly or sucked forever.

For the real hard core there was Sugar Daddy, a huge hunk of caramel on a stick. Marshalled carefully, one of these could be nibbled and licked through the previews, the Movietone News and two Woody Woodpecker cartoons. Experts could make it through an entire episode of "Lash La Rue" or "Commander Winslow of the Coast Guard" on one Sugar Daddy.

The diversity of candies sold at those old theaters seems astounding to this day. There were tiny Coke bottles with "juice" inside; fancy boxes of chocolate cigarettes, each one carefully wrapped in real cigarette paper; and bright red "wax lips" that could be worn over one's own before being eaten.

These things and many more were recalled under the stars that night by adults whose heads were full of wistful memories . . . and whose teeth were full of fillings.

— December, 1980

Cemeteries

Passing the small cemetery near Waikapu the other day, I thought how peaceful cemeteries are, and how unlike the image we have of them from literature — dark, dangerous places; "graveyards" full of skulls and ghouls.

Most island graveyards are pretty nice, and the tended ones can be beautiful — both those that are cared for privately and the big commercial ones that can afford sit-down mowers.

Even the neglected ones look good compared to what is going on around them. Traffic whipping past. Tournahauler trucks dragging tons of cane. People racing around in a frenzy trying to squeeze another buck or another deal out of this deal-weary island.

The graveyard is restful. Nobody's going to get rich in here, and nobody's going to get any poorer. If there was illness, it's over. If there were cares, they're clouds now.

The clouds float over the headstones. Tall grass bends. Flowers tap-tap in glass jars — some fresh and real, others plastic for the long haul. It doesn't matter. It's the thought that comforts.

Some graveyards are weathered, wild places on sand dunes overlooking the sea. During big swells, ghosts of salt spray drift gently among the monuments, beckoning. It's the ocean calling us back. The Bible says dust to dust, but I like spray to spray.

"Full fathom five thy father lies;
"Of his bones are coral made;
"Those are pearls that were his eyes:
"Nothing of him that doth fade
"But doth suffer a sea-change
"Into something rich and strange."

Shakespeare wrote that passage for "The Tempest," and the poet Percy Bysshe Shelley had the last three lines engraved on his headstone. He can have those. I like the first three myself, especially "Of his bones are coral made." That's a concept I can live with — the idea that we just change form.

The islands change form, too. They build themselves up out of the ocean floor like weightlifters, adding slow layers of lava.

83

Finally they bulk themselves into mighty Schwarzeneggers, thrusting skyward until their shoulders are caped with snow.

But then they wear down. They recline at last in their blue ocean plots, with just a shoal for a headstone. It's amazing to think of those islets stretching a thousand miles northwest of Kauai — Nihoa and Necker, French Frigate Shoals, Hermes Reef, Laysan, Pearl, Kure, Midway. Once towering Hawaiis and Mauis, they're just slivers of reef now. Of their bones are coral made.

I'd like to be a deep fish and swim down to the graveyard of the Hawaiian Islands. I think it might be peaceful there: no traffic, few tourists, nothing stirring but the limu. Every century or so a bubble might bloop up out of the mud and wobble toward the surface miles above, but that would be about it for action.

There's some action in land-based graveyards. In Wailuku, lei flowers are picked from a plumeria-scented cemetery at the head of Vineyard Street. Canoe teams and sunbathers park near the kiawe-shaded graveyard at Lahaina's Hanakaoo Park, and Kuau neighborhood kids shortcut through a pleasant, grassy cemetery on their way to the store.

Some resting places are the stages for major annual events. Flags snap to attention in the Makawao Veterans Cemetery, which each Veterans Day resounds with speeches and military honors. And up the mountain at Waiakoa, village children costumed as angels and prophets make an annual feast day procession around Holy Ghost Church and its small graveyard.

My favorite is the Mantokuji Mission cemetery just past Paia. I remember a night in late summer, the tail end of Obon festival season. Dancers in beautiful kimonos circle the musicians' tower, dipping and turning gracefully to the drum beats, the singers' voices.

A fat silver moon hangs over the ocean like a paper lantern. Beneath it, other paper lanterns strung through the graveyard cast soft rose, green and amber light onto the monuments. Family members picnic on woven mats among the inscribed stones, sharing this fine night with their ancestors.

Soft laughter and murmured conversation float into the warm, moonlit air around the monuments. Silver waves pulse shoreward, sea-changing the land, stirring coral and pearls. The whole night breathes life.

There are no ghosts here but the ghosts of kind regard.

— October, 1987

St. Philomena Church, Molokai. Published Dec. 26, 1975.

Mangos

Walking along the road the other day, eating a mango, I got to thinking about mangos. My first thought was: "I shouldn't be walking while I eat this."

Sure enough, a gobbet of mango splashed onto the sleeve of my favorite old Reyn's shirt. There being no water nearby, I started sucking the stain.

Cars whizzed past, full of normal people on their way home from work. I wondered if I should be sucking my sleeve in public, then thought better of it. Mangos make their own rules.

The best way to eat whole mangos, especially the giant midsummer Haydens, is while standing in the ocean. This was the preferred method in my old neighborhood, anyway. Errant youths just in from surfing would raid a seaside yard where two mangonificent Haydens, their proud limbs borne down by fruit, begged us to ease their burden.

Lightning strikes no faster. Leaving the youngest in the shallows to "guard the boards," we hopped the sea wall, raced across the lawn, twisted down the ripest fruit, and bolted back to sea before the dog could bark.

Standing in the shallows with the sun on our shoulders and mango juice trickling down our chests, we felt as close to heaven as we would probably get. In a spirit of mangonimity, we left the peels for the fish and the pits for the crabs. A final dive washed the evidence from our bodies, if not from our consciences.

In gentler hands, mangos are the currency of Hawaiian summer, the gift over the fence, the bagful left at the door or brought to work. As with bananas, their sheer bounty precludes hoarding — they have to be circulated. Mangos are the training wheels of generosity.

Perhaps because of their beauty or the hardships they entail for anyone who rakes leaves, mangos get more respect than some other island fruits — even from errant youths. I can recall guava fights, "fig" fights, rotten breadfruit fights, even ginger root wars. But for some reason we never pelted rotten mangos at each other, though they throw well and make very pleasing, Jackson Pollocktype splatters.

Speaking of art, mangos are a favorite subject of island painters, as pleasing to the palette, evidently, as to the palate. The great mango immortalizer was the 19th Century French expatriate Paul Gauguin, whose Tahitian masterpieces "Te Arii Vahine" and "Where Do We Come From, What Are We, Where Are We Going?" give mangos prominent play.

My favorite Gauguin is of a pensive woman holding a mango, her muumuu royal purple, the yellow fruit luminous in her dark hand. A print of that hung on my wall once, until the cockroaches got it.

The print is gone now, but I am again surrounded by the real thing. Earl brings them to the office. Mr. Okamoto passes them over the fence while I'm watering. They're all over the roads, especially in Kipahulu, where certain turns are literally paved with mango pits right now.

I haven't checked Lahaina lately, but that's usually the big mango town. It must have something to do with the extra sunset they get over there, since mangos seem to take their colors from the sunset. There used to be some great old mango trees in the main yard at Puamana, by the tennis courts. I hope they're still there, because I plan to surf Shark Pit soon.

In the meantime, it's good to walk along the road eating a big, juicy mango again — even if I do end up sucking my sleeve in public.

— September, 1987

Suede Jacket

Brother scribe Jon Woodhouse's wry column on his recent Bay Area travels mentioned an "upscale resale" thrift store in Mill Valley — an obscure reference to other *Maui News* readers, perhaps, but not to me.

I know the store well. It's called Family Thrift Store, and it's on Miller Avenue near Jerry's Market. I bought a jacket there once that got me in trouble.

When I moved from Maui to Mill Valley in 1984, I noticed that many successful Marin County men wore suede jackets. "I will get a suede jacket and be successful, too," I thought. But suede jackets cost hundreds of dollars more than I had.

Then one day I found a brown suede jacket in Family Thrift Store. It was made in Israel and doubtless had been worn by some successful man. The sleeves were too short and there were a couple of small stains (rust?), but to me the jacket looked beautiful. The price was beautiful, too — $20.

I couldn't wait to show it to my brother, a successful man who works in an important building in The City, as Bay Area people call San Francisco. "Look," I said, striking a sartorial pose. "And only $20!"

His brow furrowed. "That jacket will get you in trouble," he said. I just smiled, knowing that envy can take many forms.

The next day I donned my last clean shirt and jeans, slipped into my prior-owned suede jacket (silk lining!), laced up my tennies and started walking toward town to do my laundry.

With any other ensemble, I knew, the soiled canvas laundry bag slung over my shoulder might have looked dowdy, but with the suede jacket it created a bold, masculine look, a "soldier of fortune" ambience. I would be the most successful man in the laundromat.

The patrol car stopped me as I strolled through one of Mill Valley's tonier neighborhoods. I smiled at the officer and waited for him to compliment me on my new jacket.

"Set the bag down, please," he said, "and empty out the contents." So I pulled out all my dirty laundry right there in the street. Fashionable matrons slowed their Mercedeses to view the distasteful scene, then sped away. I felt like a soldier of misfortune.

"I'm sorry about this," the officer said as I stuffed my laundry back into the bag. "But we've had reports of house burglars in this area, and you looked, well, suspicious, if you don't mind my saying so. I think it's the rust stains."

"Thanks," I said. "Have a nice patrol."

By the time I reached the laundromat, the jauntiness had gone from my step, the proud jut from my jaw. I entered the building furtively, like a burglar. Instead of modeling my suede jacket for an adoring public at the bleach dispenser, I folded it up and hid it under the laundry bag.

Family Thrift Store was on my way home. I slung the laundry bag down, went inside and handed the jacket to the thrift store lady.

"Back so soon?" she said. "I thought you'd make quite an impression in that jacket."

"Oh, I made an impression all right," I said. "But I learned something about fashion today. The soldier of fortune look is definitely out."

"Oh dear," she said. "Well, how about a cashmere sweater? They're good-looking and comfortable, and they never go out of style. A very nice one came in just this morning."

It was very nice, and only $15. Made in the Orkney Islands and probably prior-owned by a powerful investment banker. The elbows were a little baggy, and there were some small holes (moths?), but to me it looked beautiful. Then I thought what the police would say, and I left it on the hanger.

— December, 1987

Happy Hour Werewolf

Thursday's demonic convergence of St. Patrick's Day with the county Liquor Commission's move to ban "happy hour" in bars has the Irishman in me thinking about alcohol.

I'm a third Irish, my dad tells me — quick to add that it comes from my mother's side. The other two thirds are English and Scottish. The English third got me through "Merchant of Venice" in high school, and the Scottish third has made me a notorious tightwad ("So tight you squeak when you walk!" as one disgusted ex put it, stalking out of Burger King on our final dinner date).

But it's the Irish third that howls on St. Patrick's Day, that throws back its shaggy head and bays for release when it sees the words: "99 cent margaritas!"

I call that third the "Happy Hour Werewolf."

The Happy Hour Werewolf clawed his way free in Sonoma, California one St. Patrick's Day, and he and I had a hell of a time loping around the plaza, stopping in each of the six bars to quaff green beer and sing Irish songs with the other werewolves:

"My name is O'Hanlon, and I've just turned 16;
"My home is in Armagh, and there I was weaned;
" 'Twas there I learned cruel England to blame;
"And now I'm a paaaaart of the patriot game!"

It was Werewolves 51, Patriots 3 by the end of that game, and the green beer looked much prettier going down. I guess it was then that I started wondering if alcohol and I were really meant for each other.

I was always a cheerful werewolf, and the bars made a comfy den, a companionable retreat from the bachelor solitude of books and laundromats and canned tuna.

Bolstered by my friends of 20 years — Bud Weiser and Marl Boro — I felt like someone else; someone funny, confident and manly, a hale fellow well met. I was surrounded by other hale fellows, greeted by name, welcomed into conversations.

There's a lot of sharing in bars: sports and work talk, cigarettes, rounds of drinks, fellowship, politics. Most of the ones I've been in, even the rough-looking ones, are generally pretty friendly. Few people go to bars to be alone.

I always enjoyed happy hour for its timing — usually at the end of the working day — and the its joyful hubbub, as cheery as a wood fire on a frosty night. But for me, happy "hour" was a misnomer, because the first one tended to multiply. I got to where I could time it out pretty well by watching my thirds drop away.

The Scotsman was the first to go, because bars foster generosity. The tightwad who came in for the dollar longnecks would end up buying rounds later on. And one night he bet $100 that the capital of West Virginia is Wheeling. ("Name any state, any state! I know every capital.") Well, it wasn't the capital that night.

The Englishman would slide away later, when lofty words like "arteriosclerosis" and "disingenuousness" sputtered out with missing syllables, or was that cylinders? And when rents appeared in the silken sails of memory.

But the Irishman hung on 'til last call, growing happier and friendlier and more soulful with each passing hour. Magical things occured. The waitresses grew more beautiful, the conversation more meaningful, the jukebox more musical. A lifetime friendship formed with what's his name.

Finally, only the Happy Hour Werewolf was left. One a.m. Chairs up on the tables, ashtrays in the sink. Time to go ... where, wolf? Home? No, not yet. The Happy Hour Werewolf knows a place open 'til two. Owooooooo!

Yes, it was a wonderful life for a werewolf, but not so good for a man — or this man, anyway. I realize everybody's different. Some people really do leave after a happy hour or two. Some people don't go into bars at all. Some don't come out.

I finally had to let it go. The werewolf was getting too big, too fast, too hard to call back. It was time to change back into a man.

I miss that scene sometimes: the people, the games on TV, the friendly roar, the music. But deep down, I know that's not all that drew me to the bars.

The werewolf's still in here. I hear him scratching and pacing around sometimes, usually at happy hour. But he's getting better. He only howls now on St. Patrick's Day.

— March, 1988

Purest Form of Entropy

"The great thing about cocaine is that it makes you feel like a new man," a friend told me once. "The only trouble is, 20 minutes later the new man wants to feel like a new man."

I could usually tell when my friend was on a cocaine binge. He would speak fiercely for many hours about entropy, a subject he never raised at other times.

I dimly remembered entropy from a college astronomy class. It's a theory that everything goes from order to chaos, like a kid's room. "The ultimate state reached in the degradation of the matter and energy of the universe" is how the dictionary defines it.

Under the influence of cocaine, my friend did indeed become a new man — the world's greatest living authority on entropy. Eyes ablaze, hands cleaving the air, he would explore the nooks and crannies of entropy until daybreak.

Every so often he'd pause to make some more powder with his little grinder, and I'd try to change the subject. "How 'bout those Celtics, huh? Did you see that shot Bird made yesterday — he looks left, fakes right, looks left, fakes left, fakes right, looks left . . . ."

"Pro basketball is exactly what I'm talking about," he'd say, peering into the grinder, scraping a little tool around in there to get more out. "Bread and circuses for the masses while the world goes to hell. It's just part of the overall pattern."

This discussion came to mind as I was rustling through the papers recently looking for some good news. It seemed like half the stories were about drugs: "Drug Supply Meeting Demand" . . . "Drugs Hurt Users" . . . "Cartel Survives Kingpin's Conviction."

The other half were about the world going to hell: ivory poachers chain-sawing the faces off African elephants, driftnets killing North Pacific sealife, the sun slowly frying us all. It sounded like entropy to me, but I called my friend to be sure. "Are you still doing cocaine?" I asked.

"Does the pope wear clean clothes?"

"Well, the reason I called is, I don't understand what's going on." I told him about the elephant faces and the driftnets, throwing in for good measure the destruction of Earth's ozone layer by aerosol propellants.

"It's all entropy," he said.

"What about Bush, and this Noriega-Contra thing? It says here that Bush visited a crack house while Reagan tried to find Noriega a nice place to retire."

"Crack is the purest form of entropy," my friend advised. "Bush should be a new man real soon."

"No, he didn't smoke it — he just went there," I said.

"The vice president should stay out of those places anyway," my friend laughed. "Crack is demeaning."

"What about Noriega?" I asked. The Panamanian dictator had been on my mind a lot. Here was a sweetheart the U.S. paid $200,000 a year — more than our own president makes — to close the cocaine nostril through Panama. Turns out the Colombians are paying him millions to keep the same nostril open.

"You gotta love the guy," my friend said. "He takes everybody's money and comes out smelling like a rose. I read that he and the Colombians set up the first Contra arms network, then flew Peruvian flake back to the U.S. on the CIA's planes. Now, that's entropy!"

"Reagan's trying to find him a place to go into exile," I said.

"All my rooms are rented out to windsurfers right now, but I'll put him on the list," my friend said helpfully. "The rent's $200,000 a year."

I rang off when he said he had to go polish his scales, but I felt dissatisfied. The "what" was clear enough — dangerous drugs were on the march all over this land. The question was, why?

I finally decided it's all part of the same pattern: the elephants killed for ivory, the ocean killed for tuna, the ozone layer killed for underarm freshness, 7th grade junkies killed so Noriega can retire and become a new man.

Entropy is all it is.

— *May, 1988*

AIDS

It's interesting watching America try to cope with AIDS.

After 20 years of "If it feels good, do it," the nation's not feeling so good about doing it any more.

The behavioral excesses of the 1970s have doubled back. Everything that was considered hip then — drugs, "free love," multiple partners of whatever persuasion — isn't looking so fine these days.

Now comes *Newsweek* to tell us that 3 million Americans are infected with the AIDS virus but don't know it yet. Fifty-five thousand already have the full disease — as many Americans as perished in Vietnam. The death rate from AIDS is 100 percent.

If that percentage doesn't change, a wall with the names of all the Americans who will die of AIDS by the year 2000 would have to be 60 times as long as the Vietnam memorial wall in Washington, D.C.

As usual, Madison Avenue is the last to get the word. While the rest of the country reels in stunned horror, the people who sell us our way of life are still hustling wanton sexuality as the best way to move acid-washed jeans.

This struck me the other day as I paged through a couple of publications my house-mate gets: *W* fashion magazine and *Interview*, a spike-hair *Rolling Stone* clone out of New York.

Both periodicals are full of pouty, brooding, half-dressed boys and girls in what appear to be the final stages of sexual exhaustion. With their swollen lips and bruised, hungry eyes, they look like vampire trainees. This is supposed to be attractive.

Hollywood and the music industry haven't caught on, either. Films, videos, records and tapes still probe America's errogenous zones, relentlessly seeking the few nerve endings not already deadened by drugs and tele-violence.

In fairness, the advertising and entertainment media are just doing what comes naturally. Sex sells, so they sell sex. If several clasped nude torsos sell perfume better than a pretty girl with a rose, the media will go with the clasped nude torsos every time.

For industries that pride themselves on being au courant,

advertising and entertainment are woefully out of date. If they were your only fix on reality, you'd think these are the swinging '70s instead of the fatal '80s. Yo, Spuds, let's party! What's going on at the Silver Bullet tonight?

This foolish nostalgia is symptomatic of our national psyche — as inappropriate as Detroit's refusal to downscale its cars, or Reagan's presidency, or "Olliemania." We're a nation with a Hula Hoop for a brain.

We think that if we just close our eyes and click our ruby slippers three times, things will once again be how they're supposed to be — America back on top, gas at 25 cents a gallon, the Japanese making nickel baseballs stuffed with newspaper.

Rock Hudson would be alive (and straight), the ozone layer intact, the Stars and Stripes flying proudly over Saigon, Nicaragua just a place our bananas come from, Coke just a soft drink, AYDS an appetite suppressant.

We have bought into this absurd fantasy for so long that we no longer recognize it for what it is — national dry rot, the beginning of the end for an obese, tottering empire founded in genocide and fueled by exploitation.

We are a nation which knows no limits. If one car is good, three must be better. If one TV is good, let's have one in every room. If sex with one partner is good, let's have 14,000 partners.

The late porn star John Holmes supposedly had 14,000 partners. He was in one sense an American hero, as important to the national libido as Ollie North is to patriotism or Jim Bakker to righteousness. Like them, Holmes was a man for the times — a personification of American excess. He died of AIDS this month.

There is a message here: Fantasies have consequences, and even America must accept limits.

The national fantasy that created John Holmes has been put through the shredder by AIDS. President Reagan can go on national TV, grin, wink, tuck us into bed with that soothing actor's voice — but he can't make AIDS go away.

Madison Avenue can give us smoldering young vampires, clasped nude torsos, acid-washed jeans at the Silver Bullet tonight — but 3 million Americans are going to be dying soon.

This might be a good time to try something else.

— March, 1988

Pennies

An announcement for the Maui AIDS Foundation's "penny crusade" got me thinking about pennies.

Pennies just pile up. Aside from the few that can ease the irksome "$3.02, please" transaction, pennies simply aren't powerful enough to be kept on "purchase alert" status. They're the buck privates of money.

Pennies never get to snap crisply out of a billfold or be palmed to a maitre d' in a swanky night spot. They don't get to light cigars, play the ponies or buy state secrets. Their biggest thrill is being run over by a train.

Pennies used to be welcomed in all the right places — at the opera, on luxury liners, in the Orient Express saloon car. Bobby-soxers tucked them into loafers when Frank Sinatra and Tommy Dorsey came to town. Now pennies can't even get into gumball machines.

So they just pile up. Mine generally wind up in a nicked monkeypod bowl on top of the dresser. They get pitched in there from my pockets at the end of each day.

When the pennies reach high tide and submerge the other things in the bowl — the spare car keys, the old St. Christopher medal — they get scooped into a plastic bucket that lives in the swirling, dustball badlands under the bed.

When that bucket fills up, it's time to switch the brain into accounting mode and spend a tedious evening poking the pennies into weird little paper tubes the bank gives out.

It would be nice if the tubes held just 50 pennies — no more, no less — but of course they don't. You have to count every coin, because the bank won't take rolls of varying lengths. But after you've counted to 50 several dozen times — and lost count several dozen more — it's amazing how closely a 49-penny roll resembles its 51-penny cousin.

The stacking and rolling process isn't entirely without pleasure. I begin by plunging my hands into the bucket, scooping up a double handful of pennies, and savoring their sheer mass. Then the coins course through my fingers like metallic grain, rattling back into their silo.

Leading Freudians claim that this sort of behavior is linked to various unsavory regressions, but I blame Uncle Scrooge comic books. He always seemed so happy diving into his coin vault from the high board, or snorkeling through silver dollars with Huey, Louie and Duey.

The plastic tub of pennies is the closest thing I have to Scrooge McDuck's treasure vault, but it did produce one minor treasure years ago — a badly worn 1909 SVDB that brought $8 at a coin shop. I wish I had that penny now. It's one of the few things I've ever owned that hasn't depreciated in value.

For a coin, the only fate worse than depreciating in value is being out of circulation. Pennies, especially, were meant to go from hand to hand, to jingle cheerfully in pockets, to bring pleasure to many users — not to languish in some dusty bucket.

Look how beautiful they are, especially the old ones. That dark, burnished brown speaks of morocco leather, Swiss chocolate, riding gloves, brandy by firelight. Our greatest president gazes thoughtfully from each penny, as if pondering the tiny word to his left: Liberty.

Perhaps inspired by that craggy profile, I finally liberated the pennies under my bed. The AIDS penny crusade was too good to pass up. Instead of prodding them into infuriating paper tubes, I just lugged them down to Artful Dodger and poured the whole lot into a bottle. The sound alone was worth it.

— May, 1988

Graduation Haircut

I was in Thelma's Barber Shop the other day, getting a graduation haircut. It was the calabash cousin of the haircut I had at my own graduation — short on the sides and back, medium on top, a little razor trim around the edges. A haircut to help a slack-key person seem serious for a while.

I don't get many haircuts, but when I do get one, I go to Thelma's. In a world of constant, puzzling, sometimes heart-breaking change, Thelma's is an island of tranquility. It says to me: Yes, those things are happening . . . but this is real, too.

There are three big leather barber chairs in Thelma's, old and deep and comfortable. There are photo calendars of Japan, well-thumbed magazines in a rack, and a ceramic cat with a paw lifted to bring business and, thus, happiness.

The shop is open on one side to the Kahului Shopping Center, itself a serene and civilized place. Reflected sunlight bathes the room, and a little cat's-paw breeze curls in around the doors, batting at tufts of hair on the floor.

The hair falls democratically from the shears — gray or white, black or brown or blond, copper sometimes. Our hair. We are men mostly, middle-aged and older, for whom a haircut is a kind of institution. The barbers dignify us with their skill, and we put ourselves in their hands.

The barber chairs face the people waiting their turns. Conversation flourishes that way, the customers relaxed, "visiting" with each other and the barbers, teasing back and forth in the island way. Sometimes the shop eases into a relaxed quiet, the snipping scissors and the sounds of birds a gentle meditation.

When the haircut is done, the barber lifts the cloth from your neck, and you check the mirror to see how you look. Because you trust the barber, and because the barber is good, you look good.

If you have a little hair, what you have is shaped with style and dignity. If you have a lot of hair, most of it goes onto the floor. You walk out feeling clean and light, a little spring in your step.

The people in Thelma's make a haircut a pleasure — the barbers kind and cheerful, the customers at ease with one another; old friends, many of them. The other day they talked about old times, swimming in the ditches as rascal kids, 40, 50 years ago.

Outside in the bright wide world, it was graduation time. In the island of Thelma's, I wondered what to write or say about this time. I was to give a graduation speech the next day, and I was scared.

What finally came to me was that graduation — for all its festivity and ceremony, its heaps of leis, its air of jubilation — is really a sad time. An exciting time, yes, an electrifying time — but one stroked as well by a feather of sorrow.

What is graduation, really? It's when we say goodbye to an island childhood. It can be a time of profound sadness, a deep movement in the heart. We are reminded then of our own rascal days, our friends and families, the world we knew.

The event says: Welcome now to the world of adults, onward and outward, excelsior! Inside our leis, we glimpse this new world in the spaces between flowers. We do feel new somehow: proud, expectant, excited by this rite of passage, this stirring embarkation.

But within our hearts, we know what graduation really is. A soft goodbye to then, to the children we have been, to our world and those who shared it. Aloha, little one I was. Goodbye.

I did not speak about this sadness at the graduation ceremony, because it crushes me. So some things did not get said. But I think of them now and offer them to you, graduates.

Some things are real and always will be. The soft fall of hair in the barber shop, the cat's-paw breeze, the dignity and trust exchanged.

When you speak with someone, look gently for the person inside, and think how that one could be you.

Trust your feelings.

— May, 1988

The Color Green

Like the sandalwood trade before it, Hawaii's sugar industry will one day fold up its plantations and move on.

Its departure will affect us in various ways. Sugar workers will be out of jobs. Those in supporting trades, from bootmakers to biplane pilots, will face layoffs. Shipping, heavy equipment and chemical firms will all feel the pinch.

For those not directly involved in Hawaii's third largest industry, its demise may be felt in another, subtler way: it will mean the end of the color green.

This thought struck me recently as I rode around Maui in the bed of a pickup truck, enjoying the blue- and green-ness of this place. For Maui is blue and green as surely as Chicago is gray and gray, or Antarctica white and white. Our blue comes from the sky and the ocean that reflects it. Our green — much of it, anyway — comes from sugar cane.

The importance of green to the state's leading industry, tourism, needs little elaboration. Many tourists come from gray cities where the only green is in window boxes and sickly trees lining smog-choked streets. They come to Hawaii because Hawaii is green.

Green is even more important to island people. We grew up in a blue and green world, and I think those colors have had a profound effect on our lives. They are the colors of nature, and they help us feel closer to nature than do our counterparts in the world's smoggy cities.

Blue and green are cool, refreshing colors that contribute to the leisurely pace of island living. We can look up from even the most demanding tasks and find blue and green on all sides, giving us a deep sense of well-being.

I enjoyed that feeling again in the bed of the pickup truck. From Waihee to Maalaea, we drove through a green landscape of cane. Across the Maui Saddle, itself a patchwork of light green and darker fields, sugar cane shimmered in a vast, sunlit belt from Haiku to Pulehu. After we passed the barren pali, sugar cane started again at Ukumehame and skirted the coast all the way to

Napili.

Watching the fields go by, I realized there is more to sugar cane than the color green. The plant that gives us sugar also shines, dances and reminds us how lucky we are to live where the sun, earth and wind combine so harmoniously.

There also is a protective quality about sugar cane. It spreads a green mantle around small Maui towns that otherwise would become suburbs: Waihee, Waiehu, Waikapu, Puunene, Paia and Olowalu. Even Wailuku and Lahaina benefit from the protective embrace of the cane fields.

The qualities that make these towns unique — their small size, rural character and slack-key lifestyle — will go when sugar goes. We have already watched it happen on Oahu, where Waipahu and Ewa were once small towns like those on Maui. The people in those towns knew each other and shared a sense of belonging to the place.

When sugar left, those towns became suburbs of Honolulu almost overnight. Used car lots, pizza parlors and high-rise apartment buildings replaced the fields of cane. The towns were connected by freeways, and they lost their identities. Green gave way to gray. Now green is giving way to gray on Maui.

It used to make me angry when politicians, developers and those who sell land for a living would say: "You can't stop progress." I hated the smug way they said it, and the way they would smile and shrug their shoulders. But I'm starting to see what they meant. You can't stop progress, because progress is what people want. It's not some evil force, but merely the sum of human choices.

On Oahu, people chose urban life over rural life. It is the same choice people have been making for 10,000 years; the same choice Maui makes every day. In the end, progress will choose pizza parlors over sugar cane and gray over green. Those who love the color green will be sad when the sugar industry folds, but we'll know its departure is the commonweal's choice.

In the meantime, 50,000 acres of cane bends and dances in the Maui wind, providing a living for many and a green tranquility for us all.

— September, 1981

Journalism
in the Schools

"Engledow and Stevens:" the boss's note began, its use of last names disquieting. "It is your turn to go into the schools. An English teacher at (name deleted because this is a small island) School wants a reporter to talk to her sixth grade classes. I'm sending both of you because I want a story and photos. Call Miss Thristle to set it up. Have fun. That is all."

For newspaper reporters, going "into the schools" can be a frightening experience for a couple of reasons. First, most of us don't like schools. If we did, we would have stayed in them long enough to qualify for some interesting, high-paying profession like investment banking or brain surgery. Instead, we went into journalism — a career that produces more than its share of brain surgery patients.

Second, it's no fun eating a school lunch. There's always something warm and gravy-covered in the middle of the tray, something cold in a little cup on the side, and a single slice of soft white bread with a pat of frozen butter that rips the bread when you try to spread it.

The schools think this is a "nutritionally balanced meal," but reporters can't eat this kind of stuff. We have to have a stale tuna sandwich and a Twinkie, preferably eaten while driving at high speed away from a school.

But the real reason we don't like to go into the schools is that we're afraid. We're writers, not talkers. We can write all day about what other people do, but if we have to talk for even 15 minutes about what we do, our knees knock, our voices shake and we have to go to the lavatory.

That's why I always try to arrive late whenever I talk to a class. Knowing that most class periods are 50 minutes long, I try to get to the school itself at least 15 minutes late ("Sorry, went to the wrong school"), then spend 15 minutes slowly circling the campus on foot, pretending to be lost ("Sorry, went to the wrong building"). By this method, the cowardly reporter can whittle his or her actual speaking time down to 20 minutes.

102

This gives 15 minutes to tell all there is to know about newspapers and reporting ("newspapers exist to sell advertising, and reporters exist to sit in the office and drink coffee") and five minutes for "question and answer."

Since most sixth graders would much rather be surfing or French-braiding their friends' hair, there usually aren't any questions from them, so the teacher has to think up two or three. The reporter can answer these by saying: "I don't know," and in a very short time can be speeding away from the school eating a Twinkie.

The day we went to (name deleted) School was different. Unfortunately, Engledow drove, so we got to the right school on the right day. I was about to slink away on foot for 15 or 20 minutes of "looking for the right classroom" when a very shapely sixth grade teacher strode up to welcome us.

Blue eyes flashing merrily, ash-blonde hair cascading down her back, her stride springy and athletic, Miss Thristle clearly was new to the teaching profession — her spirit as yet unbroken by years of spitball warfare and school lunches.

"Thanks so much for coming today," she said, shaking our hands and leading us toward her classroom. "The kids have been looking forward to this all week."

"So have we!" Engledow chirped, giving me a healthy little shot in the ribs with her elbow. "We love to talk to sixth graders, don't we, Tom?"

"Uh, yeah, love to ... spend the rest of my life here," I stammered, gazing at our hostess. "Say, Miss T., what are you doing Saturday night? I know a great little place in Lahaina where the lasagna is simply . . . ."

Fortunately for the integrity of journalism in the schools, the first period bell went off over our heads as I started to speak, shattering the soft (name of town deleted) morning like Ella Fitzgerald's voice splintering a wine glass.

". . . out of this world!" I boomed into the sudden, eerie stillness following the bell.

"I'm sorry," Miss Thristle said, shaking her fingers out of her ears. "The bell ... "

"He said the school is out of this world and he wishes he could be a lunchroom monitor here forever," Engledow put in helpfully.

I was trying to think up some snappy rejoinder (as I said, we're writers, not talkers) when we were swept into the classroom by a tidal wave of shouting, laughing, singing, stomping, book-toting, boogalooing, Valley-talking, hair-combing, locker-slamming, gum-cracking, high-fiving, hand-jiving miniature but perfectly formed human beings.

As Miss Thristle's first-period English students whizzed around us like electrons circling an adult neutron mass, their faces shining with the youthful radiance of Piero Della Francesca cherubs, I suddenly felt old, gray and meaningless. I could feel my hairline receding and my gums pulling away from my teeth.

"I think I'd better go eat breakfast now," I told Engledow. "If you don't mind taking the first two classes, I'll do the last two. Can I borrow your truck?"

"O.K.," she said. "But you better come back. We're supposed to do a story on this."

Gnawing pancakes and soft-boiled eggs at the (name deleted) Restaurant, I tried to imagine what possible account I could give of the tedious, antiquated business of newspaper reporting to two classes of relentlessly hyperactive poppers locked into a fast-forward video age.

"Reading newspapers is fun and interesting?" No, that sounded too much like a library poster, and I had seen the school library. The spines of those volumes would not often be cracked in this lifetime.

"Newspapers keep us informed about important world and national events?" Possibly, but what kind of events, what kind of world? I leafed through the morning paper: "Infant Devoured by Hogs in Oslo" ... "Chainsaw Murderer Longed for Movie Star's Love" ... "Tank Car Explosions Rip Tallahassee" ... "Government Sees No Fallout Danger in Nuclear Plant Meltdown."

No, that wouldn't do. Ninety percent of the "news" that day, as every day, was bad — much of it needlessly so. What possible good does it do us on a soft October morning on Maui, I thought, to know that a Kansas farmer lost his legs in a potato combine, or that Uruguay just had the greatest aviation disaster in its history? There was no way around it. Newspapers, as the kids would say, are "only bummahs, man."

So I decided to talk about surfing. Wiping most of the yolk off my chin, I drove back to the school and reached Miss Thristle's classroom just as the third period bell went off, starting a small rockslide behind campus and knocking several mynah birds out of the sky.

As I entered the room, Engledow twisted slowly out of a tiny student chair-desk and shuffled over to reclaim her car keys. I noticed that her hands trembled, her right foot dragged slightly, and she seemed to have developed a nasty little spasm in her left eye.

"How'd it go?" I asked cheerfully. "Did you win?"

"Nobody asked any questions," she croaked. "I had to talk for the whole two hours. And those bells kept going off. Kids were running around everywhere, jumping up and down, talking and laughing. I can't take any more."

"There, there," I soothed, noticing with alarm that her left eye had now rolled up into her head. "Why don't you have a nice little nap in the back of your truck? I'm sure you'll feel much better in an hour or two."

"Good idea," she rasped. "Say, you won't put this in the story, will you?"

"Don't worry, I won't mention it," I promised. "You have my word as a journalist."

Deeply shaken by this encounter with the shattered hulk of what had once been a robust and energetic colleague, I vowed not to repeat Engledow's mistake. I would not address the class as an adult. I would think like a sixth grader.

Taking a deep breath, I closed my eyes and chanted my old TM mantra as 36 students buzzed and swarmed like bees in the background. Then I turned to the blackboard, picked up a piece of chalk and drew a large breaking wave, with a surfer emerging from the curl. The buzzing and swarming quieted slightly.

Then I drew two monsters disco dancing and a large valentine with an arrow through it, adding the word "romance" underneath. I next printed the words "pakalolo" "cocaine" and "boogie down" on another blackboard panel.

"That should get their attention," I thought, putting the finishing touches on a drawing of Pac-Man gobbling a stick figure labeled "principal."

Sure enough, I heard delighted laughter behind me and swung around with a huge, self-satisfied grin ... to discover that the principal had taken a seat at the back of the room. I smiled sheepishly at Miss Thristle and felt my left eyeball roll up into my head.

"Good morning, sir," I mewled, backing against the blackboard and starting a weaving, lateral dance step that I hoped would erase the Pac-Man drawing. "I was just showing the class how we reporters 'boogie down' when we're off deadline."

"Very interesting," he said. "Please continue."

"As I was saying, class, the First Amendment to the U.S. Constitution guarantees freedom of speech, and this is the cornerstone of the noble profession we call journalism, a calling that numbers among its practitioners such luminaries as Heywood Campbell Broun, who has written extensively about such subjects as ..." — here I turned to the blackboard and tapped the words for emphasis — "romance, pakalolo and cocaine. His surfing and disco - monster cartoons are also widely syndicated."

"Fascinating," the principal said, steepling his hands thoughtfully. "But didn't Broun die in 1939?"

"He did, but he was decades ahead of his time," I said, wishing that I, too, had died in 1939.

It was all downhill from there. Even after the principal left, shaking his head sadly, I couldn't seem to recover my "think like a sixth grader" momentum, and I ended up talking for two full hours about journalism, reeling off one fantastic lie after another while the kids flipped through Kung-Fu magazines, braided their friends' hair and drew monster cartoons at their desks.

At last the bell erupted, catapulting the kids out of their seats like fighter pilots ejecting from a flaming F-16. The room cleared in .0006 seconds. Soon Engledow and I were in the faculty lunch room, listlessly prodding little gravy-covered mounds across our trays, pausing now and then to spear something inert from the chill cups on the side.

"How did it go?" she whispered, her eyes having returned to what for journalists passes as normal.

"Wonderfully," I croaked, tearing a ragged hole in my bread with a diamond-hard pat of butter. "I don't think we'll be invited back. The principal walked in while I was writing bad things on the blackboard. I had to talk about Heywood Campbell Broun instead.

"I'm sorry," she said, trying not to stare too openly at my still-flickering left eye. "I think I'd better drive us back to the office. You lie down in the back of the truck and rest. We'll stop somewhere and get a stale tuna sandwich."

— November, 1982

Maui in 2002

The hotel people seemed to be eating it up, but I wasn't so sure.

We were sitting in one of those windowless banquet rooms at Wailea the other week, hearing how a spiffy new Maui is going to greet 8 million tourists in the year 2002.

Now, 2002 may seem like a long time from now — a different century, even — but it's really only 14 years away. If you have a baby today, he or she will be a high school freshman when the 8 million arrive.

How many million?

As I listened to state Airports Director Owen Miyamoto and county Planning Director Chris Hart confidently outline Maui's future, I sniffed my water glass. Was the LSD in my water only, or in everyone's?

I checked the room. The members of the Hawaii Hotel Association seemed unfazed by the news that Maui's visitor count is to quadruple in the next 14 years. They smiled pleasantly, stirred their coffees. Every now and then someone brushed a crumb from a Reyn's Spooner. Their water glasses stood untouched at their places.

I decided the LSD was only in my water, so I drank the rest. Within moments, bizarre auditory hallucinations set in.

I heard Miyamoto explain how a company called Duty Free is funding a $200 million international airport near Kahului. The airport will handle the biggest commercial planes in the world, with direct flights from dozens of Pacific Rim, Canadian and U.S. cities.

I heard Hart outline plans for condominiums near Hookipa, hotels in Paia, an entire new city of 2,000 dwellings at Olowalu. Most of Maui's buildable coastline will be developed by 2002, but Kihei can be "redeveloped" to help house the 8 million.

How many million?

The hallucinations were so vivid at that point that I decided to drink my neighbor's water, too. He didn't seem to notice — just nodded amiably as Hart described the coming Olowapolis. My halluncinations, meanwhile, fixed on the number four.

Eight million tourists is four times what we have now, I figured.

That's four times as many visitors, four times as much crime, four times the traffic, four times the hotels, condos, restaurants, shopping centers, jet skis, tour boats, helicopters and bicycle thrill rides down Haleakala.

Four!

And four times as many of them means Maui will need four times as many of us. Four times the van drivers, waitpersons, lei stringers, bedmakers, shop clerks, boat captains, bellhops, construction workers, manapua makers and jet ski mechanics.

Four times four!

In my tripped-out state, it sounded like good news all around. I celebrated by drinking my other neighbor's water. If there's one thing Maui could really use right now, I reasoned, it's four times more of everything.

Four times more classrooms, four times more day care centers, four times more police and fire stations. Yes, we need quadruple sewage plants, fresh water sources, garbage dumps, power plants, public parks, harbors, hospitals and highways!

Pleased that my math was sharp even in advanced hallucinogenic delirium, I sipped more water. Any moment now, I knew, Miyamoto and Hart would tell us who is going to build all the new facilities to support the 8 million tourists and the quadrupled Maui service community.

Would it be Duty Free Shops? I wondered. No, they're already building the airport.

Chris Hemmeter? Nah — he's got his hands full endlessly cloning Versailles.

Would it be Amfac, A&B, Maui Pine, Seibu? Possibly. All have built major projects on this island, but deep-draft harbors and hospitals may not be their thing.

I waited breathlessly. But Miyamoto and Hart didn't say who's going to build Maui's new classrooms and fire stations. They just went on about how swell everything's going to be in 2002.

I was a little disappointed. It seemed like there would be something for everyone else in 2002 — 8 million warm bodies for the tourist industry, hundreds of projects for the building trades, billions of yen for Duty Free Shops. But what about the rest of us?

Then Miyamoto smiled proudly. Not only will Maui get a new airport, he said — we'll get an overpass!

That sold me right there. With its own overpass, Maui will truly be "no ka oi" for . . . .

How many million?

— October, 1988

Boat Days

The stately white cruise ship Oceanic Independence appeared out the window shortly after dawn one recent Wednesday, riding a flat blue sea toward Kahului Harbor. Far above the ship, the cloudless peaks of the West Maui Mountains glowed pink in the dawn light.

Framed by coconut trees and bathed in that soft rose light, the scene stirred memories of other ships and other times.

The Lurline, the President Wilson, the President Cleveland and other great liners plied the Pacific during the post-World War Two years, often rounding Koko Head or Diamond Head just after sunrise. The land, lying in shadow, would still be dark, and the sunlit vessels offshore seemed like images from a dream.

At midmorning, tugboats would nudge one of the huge liners into its berth next to Aloha Tower, and the Honolulu waterfront would resound with whistle blasts, the shouts of stevedores, and the rumble of lowering gangways.

The rails of the ship's promenade deck would be lined three or four deep with passengers, many waving to friends and family ashore, others drinking in their first impressions of a new home: brown-skinned men diving for coins tossed from the ship, the Royal Hawaiian band playing for a hula troupe on the dock, morning rainbows dissolving over Manoa Valley.

The ships' departures — often in the late afternoon — were more poignant. Again the band played and the hula girls danced, and again the rails were crowded with passengers, many draped so heavily with leis that their faces could scarcely be seen.

But there was always a feeling of sadness and loss on those occasions, as different from the thrill of arrival as the soft afternoon light was from the dazzling hues of morning.

The deep blast of the ship's horn at last call now seemed filled with longing, as did the passengers pressed against the rails, and their friends and loved ones in the terminal.

"Aloha! Aloha! Come back again! Goodbye!"

The calls grew fainter, the waving stronger as the ship slipped its moorings and backed slowly away, trailing thousands of colored paper streamers. The band played "Aloha Oe," and leis spiraled down from the decks to float for a moment on the water — a final, fleeting promise that the wearers would return some day.

While "Aloha Oe" was the anthem appropriate to the occasion, "Beyond the Reef" voiced that sense of longing for many who did not speak Hawaiian: "Beyond the reef, where the sea is dark and cold, my love has gone away, and my dreams grow old . . . ."

The sea did seem dark and cold at those times, in the days before hundreds of regularly scheduled airline flights could criss-cross it in hours. There was a sense of finality about ship departures, a feeling that those ashore would not see those on the ship again.

A similar finality several years ago attended the departure from Kahului Harbor of the S.S. Mariposa, then on the final leg of what was to be the last Hawaiian voyage by an American passenger liner.

The ship left Maui late one winter afternoon. A full moon hung low over the ocean, and the first great north swell of the season hammered the windward coast with 25-foot surf.

Seen from the edge of a cliff near Kahakuloa, the liner that had looked so tall and strong at dockside earlier that day now seemed toy-like against the dark, vast sea.

As the sun went down, the cliffs and the distant ship were flooded with golden light that deepened to red, then paled into violet. The ship rose and fell as the huge swells moved beneath it, and the heart was filled again with longing.

— November, 1980

110

Camp Games

Zhiew-zhiew! Zhiew-zhiew-zhiew!

At Woolworth, Pizza Factory, Apple Annie's and dozens of other places these days, the sound of intergalactic warfare can be heard above the din of cash registers and patrons' calls for another round.

These computerized space invader games, with their split-second circuitry and video readouts, seem appropriate to an age whose citizens spend much of their time gazing into video screens of one sort or another. Besides, they're good fun.

In earlier times, good fun came in the form of "Pee-Wee," "Kill Man Bag," "Fight Rubber," "Ting-A-Ling," and "Marutobi." These games and others like them were played by Hawaii plantation camp kids who made up in ingenuity what they lacked in purchasing power.

In "Pee Wee," two segments were cut from a broom handle — a four-inch piece with a beveled end that could be pushed into the ground, and a longer, hand-held piece used to strike the other one.

The object was to smack the shorter piece for distance, measuring its flight by walking the longer stick end-over-end along the ground. A variation awarded bonus points for bouncing the smaller stick with the big one before blasting it for distance.

"Kill Man Bag" was a team game and a variation of tag. Bull Durham tobacco bags — plentiful in the days of hand-rolled cigarettes — would be packed tightly with green leaves to make a projectile that would sting, but not enrage, other players.

A member of one team would be chosen in secret to carry the bag, usually hidden beneath the shirt, while the others would rush around clutching their shirts to confuse the opposing team. At length the smack of the "Kill Man Bag" on exposed flesh would reveal the thrower's identity, to the chagrin of the opponent who had been hit by the bag.

The object of "Fight Rubber" was even simpler: to inflict sudden, intense pain on the opponent. The weapon of choice was a gun stock fashioned from wood and notched at both ends. Black rubber tubing was stretched between the notches.

"Fight Rubber" players would stalk each other around the camps like bounty hunters, their movements marked by the snap of the rubber and the screams of their victims, who included younger brothers and sisters if no one else would play.

"Ting-A-Ling" was a variation on hide-and-seek in which the "base" was a can filled with pebbles. If one of the hiders could get back to the can before the "it," the "ting-a-ling" of the pebbles would signal the others to come out of hiding.

Games reserved primarily for girls included jacks, bean bags and simply "beans." The latter involved combing the camps and canefields for certain highly-prized beans or seeds. Koa seeds would be gatheriung into a piece of cloth and sewn up as bean bags. Elephant pod beans would be husked in a bucket and tossed into the air by tens, the winner being the girl who caught the largest number of her own beans.

Another girls' game was "Marutobi" ("circle hop"), a hopscotch variation in which large circles would be drawn in the dust to make a sort of snowman-like figure connected by lines.

Players would scatter a handful of polished glass "kinis" onto the circle area before backing off some distance and then dashing toward the circles. Only the circles without kinis were "safe" to jump into. Players would hop among these on one foot while gathering up the bits of glass from the adjoining circles.

Home-made camp toys included tissue paper kites flown with thread, samurai swords made of panax wood that could be drawn from panax bark scabbards, and ingenious little cars made from chopsticks, crayons and spools of thread.

These vehicles had notched spool "wheels" mounted on color crayon axles and a chopstick chassis. The engine was a twisted rubber band. Built properly, these sturdy little creations could whiz along the ground and even climb over low obstacles, their builders attest.

The cars, the camp games and barefoot afternoons under the Elephant Pod tree are memories now, to be shared with the grandchildren when the TV is on the blink.

— November, 1980

Thanksgiving

Tutu used to drive out for Thanksgiving in her green Buick. She'd beep the horn, and my brothers and I would run out to see if she'd made rice pudding that year or tapioca. My middle brother hated rice pudding because of the raisins, so some years she brought both.

She was very spry in those days and could easily handle whatever she had brought — the one or two puddings, a wicker basket of ceremonial tablecloths and napkins, and a ceremonial bottle of Johnnie Walker. She let us carry the other things, but Tutu held to the Prohibition wisdom that liquor was not to be entrusted to those who might drop it.

We formed a procession from the Buick to the kitchen. There Tutu's daughter, our mom, was conducting a symphony of fragrances with her spoon: wild rice, candied yams, peas simmering with water chestnuts, gravy for the mashed potatoes. The little window in the oven door yielded a glimpse of a browning turkey, but Tutu soon enforced the holiday Prohibition against useless boys underfoot, and we saw no more.

My brothers and I weren't strictly useless at Thanksgiving — unfocused might be a better word. We had already done some work, albeit languidly. We had raked and mowed the yard, strung leis for the guests, and polished black stuff off the silver tureens used only at Thanksgiving and Christmas.

We liked to grumble about the tureens. "Why do we need these? We never use these any other time. This black stuff won't kill anybody."

We figured that when our time came to host Thanksgiving, we'd rule that no kids would have to polish anything, but could play street football until dark or until dinner was ready, whichever came first.

The street in our neighborhood was good for football, because it was straight, wide and sparsely traveled. Our "field" was the stretch of asphalt in front of Alan Short's house, the neighborhood's geographical 50-yard line. On Thanksgiving, kids from the north end of the street would play "The South," which is what somebody told us they did on the Mainland.

The plays were simple, because each team only had two or three guys who could throw, catch or run worth a nickel. The rest of us served mainly to fatten the huddle and to collide with the other team's huddle-fatteners.

"Johnny, you go long," the quarterback would whisper, tracing the route on the tarmac with his finger. "Rocky, go out five yards and cut toward the Wilders' car. Everybody else, block!"

After a couple of hours of blocking, either The North or The South would win, and we'd go home to rake the yard or polish tureens. Not long after that, tutus would start pulling up in Buicks and DeSotos all over the neighborhood, the cooks would start their gravies, and Thanksgiving dinner would officially begin.

Every family had its own style — some went paper-plate casual or ate buffet-style on the patio. We always went formal so that Tutu's ceremonial tablecloth would get used.

With the table set, the candles lit, and everybody standing politely behind their chairs, some kind of prayer was called for. This was a rare and exciting occurrence at our house, where prayers were heard about as often as offers to polish the silver. I don't mean by this that we took the name of the Lord in vain — we just didn't take it out of vain much, either.

Since our father had provided the turkey and would have to carve it, since our mom had cooked it and worried about it, and since Tutu and her elderly sisters were our guests, the prayer usually fell to one of us boys.

"Dear Lord, we, uh, we thank you for bringing us all together here today." Pause. "This Thanksgiving day." Pause. "We thank you for this wonderful turkey and cranberry sauce, mashed potatoes and even the oyster stuffing. Thank you for keeping us all alive from last year. And for letting The North win today." Long pause.

"America!" another brother would hiss.

"And thank you, Lord, for America, where the Pilgrims landed so long ago. They first ate turkey and cranberry sauce in your name Amen."

With that, we would pull out the chairs for the ladies, who would sit. Then we would sit, our father would carve, and we would all politely pass dishes of food clockwise around the table until everybody had everything. Then we would eat, pause for breath, and eat some more.

During pauses, Tutu and her sisters would say: "Why, I couldn't possibly" before accepting some more of whatever it was they couldn't possibly. We brothers were under no such constraints. We just put our heads down and kept eating, as though the volume consumed was somehow important in our standing with the Lord.

Afterward, we cleared the table and went into the kitchen to do the dishes and see what pies had come with the great aunts. Pumpkin was mandatory, but apple and mince pie often showed up, too. One of the aunts — Aunt Helen, I think — liked a slice of cheese on her pie. My brothers and I considered this deadliest poison. In our view, pie slices were meant to be platforms for whipped cream, with small continents of ice cream deposited alongside.

While we did the dishes and discussed the merits of pie, the grownups idled at the dinner table with Johnnie Walker, telling stories and laughing over old times. When the great aunts started talking about riding to Kauai on the interisland steamship, that was mom's signal each year to start the coffee.

Those Thanksgivings are gone, now, and so are the great aunts. Tutu turned 90 this year and went into the hospital with pneumonia. She had to stop driving, so her old green Buick sits outside my place now. Dad is very sick, too, and the brothers are scattered to the four winds.

It's a different holiday these days. I'll go home today to see my parents and pay Tutu a visit, if she's up to it. The tureens will stay in the cupboard, and if we eat dinner at home, it will be a modest one, paper-plate casual.

Now, before I leave, it seems important to think about what Thanksgiving is and what it's not. It's not oyster stuffing, street football, water chestnuts or mince pies; not turkey or candles or Tutu's rice pudding. It's not America or the prayer.

It's the people. You miss the ones who aren't here and cherish the ones who are.

— November, 1987

Rats

The rats were gnawing and squeaking around inside my wall the other midnight, so I pounded on the canec a few times to let them know I was home. They quieted right down.

The rats in Hawaii are generally pretty respectful, not like those 26-pound rats I read about in the paper a few issues back. Running around in Oman or Surinam or someplace, terrorizing the populace. Some kind of nuclear rats, I think they were.

We just have regular rats here: plump, sleek and easy going. Easy going through your screens and groceries, anyway. My policy with the rats is live and let live — they live on their side of the wall; I live on mine.

It wasn't always that way. I used to hate rats as much as the next guy. It's un-American not to hate rats. Our national perception of them is that they live in sewers, have red eyes and razor teeth, and are covered with slime.

Island rats aren't like that at all, at least the ones I've seen. They are a handsome gray or brown color like Frank Sinatra's hats. Their pelts are dry, shiny and healthy-looking, and they're very athletic. They are the Houdinis of the animal world, squeezing into impossible spaces and making breathtaking escapes by guile and gymnastics.

I watched 13 rats escape from a big cardboard box in Kuau one time. I had dragged the box out of a backyard storage shed in preparation for a move. I opened the flaps, then jerked back reflexively as a huge brown rat rocketed out of the box, flew through the air and hit the ground running. It streaked for the panax hedge and was gone.

No sooner had the first one disappeared than a second, a third, a fourth and a fifth shot out of the box and raced away across the yard. Soon rats of all sizes were flying out of the box like popcorn. I stood frozen in horror by this un-American spectacle. All I could do was count the rats: 13. The packing box that had been their home was unuseable, but I felt better about the move.

That was the most rats I've seen at one time, but the most memorable rat was the big gray bomber who used to run around

Gecko Mecca, an old hippie house at Waiehu Beach. I was a pretend hippie at the time, and Gecko Mecca seemed a fine place to learn about crystals and spirulina.

One night, after chanting in the hot tub with people named after various kinds of weather, I entered my little room, flicked on the light, and found myself whisker-to-whisker with the Gray Bomber. Never having been that close to a huge, live rat before, I slammed the door, trapping us both.

It was a tossup as to which of us was more scared. I snatched up some blunt object — my underwater flashlight, I think — and gestured menacingly at the big rodent. The rat fixed me with a steely gaze and stayed right where it was. It knew a pretend hippie when it saw one. Finally I advanced, thinking to corner the rat and club it . . . if it didn't leap at me and tear out my throat first.

The rat raced around the room, desperately seeking its exit hole, while I stalked it from what I judged to be safe throat-tearing distance. This went on for a minute or so, and we watched each other the whole time. The rat was terrified and panting — I could see its sides heaving — but it never lost its head. Finally it scuttled up a wall and crossed the room by running upside-down along a ceiling beam, squeezed through a tiny hole high up the far wall and was gone.

I moved shortly afterward. My chakras couldn't take it.

My "rat karma" — as the people named after weather might have called it — wasn't through with me yet, though. My next room was a converted tool shed near Pukalani that rats had inhabited long before renters. The rats stayed in between the walls, so that was good — I didn't see one the whole year. But I heard them chewing the walls at night, chittering and nittering happily among themselves.

I'm still not crazy about rats, but these and other close encounters convinced me that they're not the evil baby-hunters so chillingly portrayed in "Lady and the Tramp." They're just critters, trying to get by in a world of cats and traps and scared guys with flashlights.

— September, 1987

Admission Day

In dressing for Admission Day this year, I wanted the right look, something both festive and funereal to mark Hawaii's strangest holiday. I settled on a black aloha shirt, black orchid in the buttonhole.

Admission Day always leaves me with mixed feelings. I know I'm supposed to be proud to be a full-fledged American, with the right to bear arms and vote for my own governor and legislators. And I am grateful to be a citizen of the first nation under God to mandate liberty and justice for all.

It's the other stuff I'm not sure about: The 7 million tourists a year, the Star Wars base in Kihei, the $45 bag of groceries.

I wasn't old enough to vote in the 1959 statehood election, but I probably would have voted yes. Just about everybody did — the final ratio was 17-to-1 for statehood. We were well primed for it. We waved little American flags in school, and the 49th State Fair reminded us each year of our intended destiny, though oil-rich Alaska got there first.

Hawaii was rich in aloha in those days, so we became the "Aloha State." And our relief in being "First Class Citizens Now," as one newspaper headlined, was palpable. Statehood was the real thing, the cure for a "subtle inferiority of spirit" that John Burns detected in a people too long suppressed.

The power to elect their own governor and representatives was a tremendous symbol to people who for generations had been told when to jump and how high, where they could live, what they could buy. That's worth celebrating on Admission Day in the land of the free.

Then why the ambiguity? Why is the anniversary of what many consider Hawaii's finest hour a holiday with no parade, no music, no laughter? There was music and laughter to spare on March 12, 1959, when word came from Washington that Congress had finally passed the statehood bill.

Sirens went off, church bells rang, and they let us out of school early. It seemed like everybody ended up in Waikiki, where stage bands played from platforms set up in front of the Moana, the

118

Surfrider, the Royal Hawaiian. Kalakaua Avenue was closed to traffic, and couples waltzed in the spinning street.

An "international bonfire" lit the sky over Sand Island, and Navy destroyers split the night with rocketfire and thundering cannons. A Chinese dragon danced to a 10,000-firecracker salute. It was a major party.

The celebration continued for several months as Hawaii peeled off its familiar old "T.H." work khakis and palaka shirt and got measured for the shiny new suit of statehood. Hawaii then was like a shy, sweet, country boy who had slicked his hair and put on black shoes to meet his contract bride, Tourism, and her wealthy parents, the United States of America.

Imagine his surprise, and ours, when the very experienced bride-to-be sashayed up the walk in spike heels and a tight, slit skirt, waving an ebony cigarette holder and croaking commands in a voice hardened by Vegas and vodka.

"Where is this bumpkin?" she rasped. "Let's get this damn thing over with. I need a martini."

The rest is history. The wedding was held, and the gawky Territory of Hawaii became the flashy Fiftieth, the Al-o-o-o-o-o-ha! State. The new suit never did fit and the black shoes pinched, but we got used to them. The abrasive, demanding ways of our new in-laws and the 49 Mainland relatives were hard to accept at first, but there was no going back. We were family now.

It's easy to blame statehood for everything that happened next — the money craziness, the 7 million tourists, pakalolo, skyscrapers, traffic jams, hippies, hookers, heroin.

But all that would have happened anyway. It might have taken a little longer if Hawaii had stayed a territory or even if the new state had chosen a different name — "The Sea Urchin State," maybe, or "The Centipede State" — but things still would have turned out the way they did. It's history.

So there are some mixed feelings on Admission Day. There is pride, certainly, in being First Class Citizens Now, citizens of a state that is a model of equality, humanity and progressive governance.

And there is satisfaction in progress and prosperity, especially to those whose grandparents and great-grandparents could only dream of those things.

But there's a little sadness today, too, and a little shame. The sadness is for the shy, sweet, country boy; the shame for what we let him become.

— August, 1987

Thrift Chic

If "clothes make the man," as some (probably well-dressed) person once said, then I am a thrift store.

Right now I'm wearing my charcoal gray Pierre Cardin thin wale cords, purchased for 33 cents at Ka Lima O Maui during the big "3 for $1" pants sale.

The Pierre Cardins are very comfortable and exactly the right length, but their original owner was a bit beefier than I am, so I bought a 50 cent belt to hold them up. It was tough paying more for the belt than for the pants, but "thrift chic" has its own rules.

To complete my ensemble, I am wearing à "Customline" permapress shirt bought from the Salvation Army for a dollar. It's butter yellow with accent stripes in green, red and blue, and there are no visible rust stains.

Do I look good in this outfit? Let's put it this way: If I walked through Liberty House right now, the salesladies would black out in horror and pitch forward onto the carpeting, turning as they fell to avoid wrinkling their outfits.

I don't care. I've never put much stock in personal appearance — it detracts from a person's finer qualities, and it costs too much. A cotton aloha shirt sells for $50 these days. A nice pair of slacks costs $80. New shoes? Forget it.

In my book, money is for beer, records, food, gas and rent. Clothes you can get for free.

Zoris are the easiest, if you're not picky about getting a matched pair. Walk any Maui shoreline after a good storm and you'll find all kinds of zoris, most with thongs intact. You might even find a left and a right. Ball caps also float ashore from time to time. I once found and proudly wore a red and gold one that said "USC Football."

Pants and shirts are harder to find, but if you keep your eyes open, you can sometimes spot these garments lying by the roadsides. They blow out of young tourists' rent-a-cars when the young tourists are riding around under the influence of mushrooms.

It's hard to get a good fit with these roadside clothes, though, unless you're built like a young tourist. If you have a regular island build, you might do better at a thrift store. You can still wear other people's clothing — you just pay the store a nominal fee for folding and hanging the clothes and organizing them in some way.

Most thrift stores are organized around a single huge room full of old clothes, surrounded by old furniture, old lamps, old books, old magazines, broken toys and religious ikons. There is usually another room in the back, half the size of the main room but piled with twice as much stuff. This is the more tempting area, because its goods haven't been picked over yet, but the thrift store employees guard it like imperial dragons. That's where their stuff is.

Back in the main room, the old clothes are grouped roughly by sex. There are always far more women's clothes than men's, because women must stand before their closets for 20 minutes each morning flinging outfit after outfit over the backs of chairs. Kids' thrift clothes also sell briskly, as nothing makes less sense than buying brand new outfits for these walking pituitary glands, some capable of growing six inches between breakfast and lunch.

For adults, timing is very important at thrift stores. The best time for men to shop is in winter or early spring, when rich guys are donating their old clothes to charity for the tax deductions. Lots of "Polo" T-shirts and Harris Tweed smoking jackets show up then.

For women, the best time to shop thrift is after some trendy "makeover consultant" has hit town. Armed with color palettes and swatches of fabric, these cosmetic astrologers can separate the autumns from the winters and the spring-tending-toward-summers from the summer risings.

Women who have "had their colors done" are a veritable Mississippi of rejected clothes, most of which go to the friends who urged them to have their colors done. The rest of the rejects go to thrift stores, where they are never seen by makeover consultants, who can afford designer clothes.

I've got nothing against designer clothes, mind you, or well-dressed people. There are several well-dressed people right here at *The Maui News*, and they are forever getting compliments on their clothes and good taste. I must confess, I envy them that. I'm still waiting for someone to compliment me on my Pierre Cardin thin-wale cords.

"What handsome, comfortable-looking pants!" I imagine them saying.

"Pierre Cardins," I would reply airily, fitting a perfumed cigarette into a thin ebony holder.

"I love how you've gathered them at the waist with that darling belt," they would continue. "You're so clever that way."

"Cette elegance nuage, ce n'est pas la meme chose," I would

reply, smiling graciously in French.

This conversation only goes on in my head, though. The only time anybody ever commented on my appearance was the day I wore my finest outfit — the wheat-colored suede shirt with red piping (L.L. Bean, $2, Ka Lima) and the pleated-front Ivy League khakis (Brooks Brothers, $1, New-to-You).

I was proud of this ensemble and checked myself out carefully in the mirror before going to work. I had to admit that, for me, I looked very sharp. My socks even matched.

My sartorial efforts did not go unnoticed. As I sauntered into work, the company's snappiest dresser turned in her seat and gave me a long, appraising look.

"Thrift store having a sale?" she said.

— February, 1984

Island Autumn

There's so much . . . .

The weekend brought perfect weather, and the season's first north swell rolled into Hookipa like a birthday present from the blue.

At Kepaniwai Park, hundreds attended parties and outdoor weddings. The bright air filled with Hawaiian music, laughter, the savory sizzle of linguesa. High above, the mountains were as clear as an eye.

Quieter festivities drew a band of riders to the Ulumalu roping arena, where the early afternoon light was as sharp and soft as a clipped mane. On Sunday morning, two white canoes shot past the shorebreak at Kuau Bay and stroked off toward Maliko.

Later, the sails of windsurfers off Mama's Beach reminded me of autumn. Maybe it was the colors — orange, red, maroon and green flicked across the sea like leaves dancing in an October wind.

The sun was as hot, the ocean as inviting as on any summer day, but some subtle change had occurred. The light seemed a little softer, the colors a little richer, the wind as quick as a kiss goodbye.

Autumn. The great world turns now on its shoulder like a sleeper nearing dawn. The drowsy blanket of summer falls away, and winter waits, thin as a sheet, chill as the morning air.

The dreams of summer — flocks of birds, shoals of fish, flowers spilling from full trees — begin to shimmer and fade.

Now the dreams of winter stir, gathering like whales in the deep. Rising, rising, streaking upward, they will breach and boom like cannons, reminding us of greatest force.

But not yet. Now we lie in island autumn, a hammock slung between the seasons.

In other places, autumn is a season of its own — the time when Jack Frost paints the leaves, when pumpkins and Indian corn brighten fading fields.

In other places, the October air is scented with fallen apples, mown grass, the smoke of burning leaves. The wind cuts there,

123

and ice forms in the hollows of deep shade.

There, fall is a red and golden time, following the greens of summer, preceding winter's blacks and whites. At its peak, autumn turns the hills to glowing beds of coals. Standing in their midst, one cannot point to any tree or any grove of trees as the most beautiful. The whole earth throbs with color.

In the towns within the trees, people walk briskly, breath becomes visible, hands and noses redden. Scarves, boots and coats wait in the halls. White-painted church spires catch the departing sun, and geese fly south in distant vees.

There is a sadness also. The knowledge that winter is coming — that the sky will turn to iron and that no green, gorwing thing will appear for months — makes autumn doubly precious and its passage poignant.

The light of autumn is a candle, its voice a cello, its wine a Burgundy. Its hair is auburn shot with silver, its body slender as a birch canoe. Its heart is a forest pool at twilight — dark and deep, as still as glass.

Too sad for me. I like this island autumn better. Swinging gently in its hammock, I see the great blue backs of waves to come, feel a drizzle in the wind.

Soon the iwa birds will fly. Rains will green the land as storm clouds walk the coast from Hana, tall and proud as any royal court. Baldwin Park will flood, and heedless rent-a-cars will stall coil-deep in the Red Sea of its parking lot.

The county fair will come and go, making its final stand at the Kahului Fairgrounds. There'll be some autumnal sadness around that, especially for those whose memories of the fair run generations deep. There will be other fairs, but no others like this one.

After the fair, high school football will resume. The stadium will rock and roll with cheerleaders, players, parents, kids and two brass bands. And Bull Kaya, the voice of Maui autumn, will put the ball "just a manapua away" from first down.

— October, 1988

Winter Whales

It is winter — the season of storms and whales and high surf; the best time to be in the islands. There's a crackle in the air and a champagne light. Salt collects on car windshields, and a snap of ozone drifts from crushed waves.

It's not for everyone. The resort people prefer an endless summer — their idyll is a glossy brochure of flat blue horizons and oiled bodies on beach chairs. They could be anywhere.

I like this island in winter. Endless summer here is vexing, a season swollen with glare and dust, buffeted by winds that bring no rain. The nights are sullen, the days as hard and bright as Miss Hawaii's fingernails.

And there are no whales.

Whales are the power of island winter, as dark as iwa birds coasting on thunder, as huge as lightning striking the sea. They are the great waves made flesh, the song of ancestors, the sounding and wounding of the heart.

After summering in Alaska, they boom up out of deep November to sing and calve in these warm bays. Their breaths puff the channel off Lahaina's pali, and their flukes pound the shallow lees. We're lucky to be so near them.

One winter morning I was out watering the lawn when I heard a cannon go off. I ran around to the ocean side of the cottage I rented at Maalaea. A huge black tail stood out of the ocean about 150 yards offshore. As I watched, the great flukes spanked down on the water.

There was silence for a moment, then an echo from the sloped beach way in by the condos: "Boom!" The flukes rose and pounded again: Spank . . . boom! Spank . . . boom! Spank . . . boom! Twenty times at least. It was like a naval artillery salute.

Finally the pounding stopped. The whale rolled onto its back and stroked something in the water with its long pectoral fins. Then two whales were visible, one smaller. They lazed there for an hour, the big one on its back, before swimming slowly away toward the Maalaea breakwall.

I might have seen a whale's birth that day, but I'll never know.

I thought briefly about swimming out for a closer look but decided against it, since I wasn't part of the immediate family.

The word "whale" is Welsh, I'm told, derived from "wheel" for the distinctive wheeling or rolling motion a whale makes as it surfaces to breathe. It was a Welsh poet, Dylan Thomas, who first linked whales and winter in my mind.

One winter our ninth grade English teacher played a record of Thomas reciting "A Child's Christmas in Wales." It was warm in Honolulu, but we closed our eyes and rode that dark, rich voice to a place where snow fell on the waves and "the whole of the sea was hilly with whales."

Another whale poet was Robinson Jeffers, who built a strange stone castle of a house in Carmel and watched the California gray whales from his lofty turret. He decided they had instrinsic value aside from his poetry:

"All the arts lose virtue
"Against the essential reality
"Of creatures going about their business
"Among the equally
"Earnest elements of nature."

If I were a poet, I'd warn the whales away from Maui. It's getting pretty crazy out there, with jet skis and parasail boats slashing the ocean, and snorkle armadas racing to Molokini each morning to drag anchor and cloud the "marine reserve" with urine and bread sops.

The whales should also keep a sharp eye for bogus "research teams" who tear around in Zodiacs and small planes, for photographers whose probing close-ups ring cash registers, and for "whale watch" boats flying the bright green burgee of greed.

The whales come here to reproduce. I'm reasonably certain they can do that without being photographed, interfaced with, sung to, danced with, interviewed, "adopted," windsurfed up to, kayaked out to and jet skied over.

Maui is not a theme park yet. This is still a real place, with storms and waves and winter whales "going about their business among the equally earnest elements of nature."

I think we should leave them alone.

— November, 1987

Real Trees

If we ever need a reminder that this is an island state, Matson's annual Christmas tree announcement will serve.

"The principal shipment of Christmas trees for Hawaii consumers will arrive in Honolulu the morning of December 3 aboard the Matson Navigation Company's S.S. Kauai," this year's announcement said.

The Oahu trees, mostly Douglas firs, were to leave Seattle in 255 refrigerated containers, following an earlier shipment of 75 containers bound for the Neighbor Islands aboard the S.S. Maunalani. At about 400 to the container, that's more than 130,000 real Christmas trees.

By "real" trees I mean evergreens that have a spicy, piney scent and drop needles on the carpet: Douglas firs, blue spruces, Noble firs and Monterey pines, basically. Pretend Christmas trees include Norfolk Island pines, which are the right shape but don't smell like Christmas, and cypresses, which smell good but are shaped like Boy George's hair.

The real trees have to be cut weeks ahead of time, sized, packed into Matson containers and shipped across the ocean to Hawaii. Here regular people, many with small children tugging on them, will peel off big bills for a tree that by Christmas may be as bare as Little Beach.

Why do we go to such lengths to get real trees every year? I think we do it for the smell. Smell is the sense that most keenly triggers memory, and memory is the engine that drives Christmas.

This is especially true in Hawaii, where the fragrance of Douglas firs isn't an everyday scent like it is in the Pacific Northwest. There, if you smell fir trees, you think: "Oh, fir trees." Here, if you smell fir trees, you think: "Christmas!"

Just pinching a few Douglas fir needles under one's nose can release an intoxicating rush of holiday associations here: rainy pavement reflecting strings of colored lights, friends and family arriving for holiday parties, poinsettias in gold foil, triple carnation leis and slow dancing at school proms.

I think most Christmas memories are fixed very early. Babies gaze raptly at shiny ornaments and colored lights, feel the stirring of holiday excitement in the house, crinkle wrapping paper and ribbons, gnaw on packages, hear carols and taste eggnog for the first time — all within sniffing distance of a fir tree.

That fragrance is one of the constants of Christmas. It follows shoppers through crowded malls, greets worshippers when they duck out of blustery Kona weather into the parish hall, or football fans when they duck into a tavern. And it welcomes many back home at the end of hard days.

All along, that fir tree smell triggers a slow time release of memories, many of them pleasant ones from childhood. That's because Christmas is most intense in childhood, when everything is new, enchanting and mysterious. As we fall away from childhood, each Christmas offers less mystery and more memory. I think that's why we want the Matson trees.

At some point in the falling away, Christmas changes for kids. It's one of the developmental milestones in American life — when you first realize that it wasn't Santa who ate the cookies you set out on Christmas eve.

I don't remember discovering "the truth" about Santa, but I remember when Christmas changed. I was 4 or 5, living in Aina Haina on Oahu. I woke up one midnight deep in December. Images from Christmas stories tumbled through my mind like clothes in a dryer — candy canes, reindeer, Santa Claus, elves.

Excited and confused, I went to the window. The night was still and clear; the moon so bright that the lawn seemed to lie beneath a deep, crisp, cool, silvery blanket.

Snow! I thought. It had snowed for Christmas!

I clutched my blue rabbit and raced outside, my heart surging with joy. But there was no snow. The tropical air was as warm as always; the lawn just a lawn; I just a puzzled boy standing in the moonlight.

Christmas changed that night; it lost some magic. But it gave me something in return. Of all the snows I've seen since then, none has ever been as bright or cool or silver as that memory.

— *November, 1987*

Liberated sumo, Wailuku. Published June 16, 1976.

Juggler and fans, Art Maui. Published March 15, 1982.

"Toilet Bowl," Kahului Airport. Published Jan. 9, 1976.

Paddlers off Hale O Lono, Molokai. Published Oct. 21, 1975.

Siloama Church, Kalawao, Molokai. Published Dec. 26, 1975.

Auntie Clara Ku at Kawakiu, Molokai. Published July 7, 1975.

PEOPLE
AND PLACES

Old friends, Puunene Reunion. Published Aug. 22, 1983.

Puunene Reunion

Once upon a time, before statehood and tourists and television
and prosperity and pakalolo and Tom Selleck and Pizza Hut came
to Hawaii, there were just people.

They lived in places like Puunene. The earth was red, the sky
was blue, and the sugar cane bent in the wind all day. The people
lived a simple life, those days. They worked, they went to school
and to church, they raised families, they shared what they had,
they played paiute on their front porches.

In Puunene and other plantation towns, the people lived in
"camps" with names like Spanish B, Alabama and Young Hee.
Everybody knew everybody those days, because the camps were all
chop suey. Hawaiians lived next door to Filipinos, and Filipinos
lived next to Portuguese, and Portuguese lived next to Japanese.

All the people used to walk around in the camps, because nobody
had cars. The kids never even had shoes. Well, they had — but they
only wore twice a year. Once for the county fair, and once for
graduation from Puunene School 8th grade.

The school was so important. They all went there, like it or not.
They learned to write and read and obey the teacher, and they
played milk covers and "ini quatro" marbles on the packed dirt
under the monkeypod trees. Then they graduated and went away —
some to Honolulu and the Big Island, some to the Mainland, some
to Wailuku and Kahului. They fell in love and married and had
families of their own, but they left their class pictures behind.

The Puunene reunion was held last weekend at Puunene School,
and most of the class pictures were up on the wall there, in the long
cool hallway of the administration building.

How proud they looked, those young graduates of long ago. The
boys wore crisp, starched shirts, new haircuts and their fathers'
ties. The girls wore full-length white gowns with orchid corsages,
and the shoes on their feet were all crossed the same way — right
over left, as the photographer instructed.

It was with the class pictures that many people started their
reunion weekend on Friday. Standing in the dim hallway, they
gazed at the faces of the people they had known and been 40 years

139

before. Then, bumping another person gazing at the same class picture, they turned, stared for a moment, and . . . .

"Angie! Angie DeCambra!"

"Yes, that's me. Are you . . . ?"

"Margaret Manalo!" the other woman said, pointing to her 8th grade face in the yellowing class photo. "Only now I'm Margaret Young, from Honolulu. I used to live down from your house when you folks lived on the tar road. I was a cheerleader before."

"Oh, I remember you!" Angie laughed, and they embraced before returning to the picture. "Look how thin we were! It seems like all the thin ones got fat, and all the fat ones got thin! I was five feet four and weighed 85 pounds. But then I married my husband, and you know what they say: You go into a good pasture, you gain weight!"

"Remember that big mango tree by the tournahauler road?" Margaret asked. "We were so afraid to pass by there at night, because they told us there was a big man who lived in the tree, and he would come down and choke us. But we used to sneak out anyway! We'd steal bacalayos and cerizos from our house and go roast them on a stick at the bath house . . . ."

"Oh, we never could go out at night," Angie said, regretfully. "There were 13 in our family, and our mother made us stay inside and say our prayers."

"Oh, that's right," Margaret sympathized. "You couldn't be naughty like us. But I liked you the best of all your brothers and sisters, because you always had a kind word to say."

"Thank you," Angie said softly.

On Saturday, all the folding chairs and hibachis and coolers came out, and a thousand people spread out on the shady school lawn to talk story and enjoy the official reunion program.

A group of old-timers with guitars and ukuleles played hapa-haole songs, and there were ethnic dances by beautifully costumed Japanese, Okinawan and Filipino troupes. When it came time for the "Tanko Bushi," a hundred onlookers joined the regular dancers to perform the graceful, age-old steps of the Japanese circle dance.

The soda and chow fun booths did a brisk business, and the reunion T-shirts sold out so fast a second printing had to be ordered. One of the first designs to go showed a half-dozen naked, brown-skinned kids scrambling out of an irrigation ditch as a whip-wielding luna approached on horseback.

"That was the camp policeman, Joe DeLima," said Richard Marks of Molokai, one of many former Puunene kids who swam naked in the ditch. "We used to go into the bushes like a streak when we saw him coming. That whip would crack, and you'd think he was going to take your head off, but he never touched a kid with it — just scared the hell out of us."

As part of Saturday's program, DeLima's son Abel reenacted that historic scene for television news cameras at the very same irrigation ditch. A dozen youngsters — wearing bathing suits this time — swam up the ditch toward the narrow footbridge, and DeLima dutifully chased them out with his horse.

That was supposed to be it, but the rascal in some Puunene kids never dies. Out of the crowd dove, fully-clothed, Rosie Moniz, Lucy Torres, Nita Cabiles and Priscilla Ah Yen — and the four laughing, middle-aged women hit the water like human cannonballs.

"Puunene! Puunene! Yea, Puunene!" they yelled from the ditch. Soon Charles Recamara and Lawrence Martins joined them, the latter explaining that he had come all the way from the Mainland just to swim in that ditch again.

On Saturday night, there was a luau for 3,000 and a variety show that featured hula dancing, a moving tribute to former Puunene swim coach Soichi Sakamoto, and some wickedly funny stand-up comedy from Pachi Tsukano, who concluded his act by getting several former cheerleaders up on stage for a dimly remembered chorus of the school fight song "Puunene No Ka Oi."

Old boyhood friends with nicknames like "Hard Head" and "Ice Cream" and "Five Cent" strolled around the party with their arms around each others' shoulders, and "Puunene girls" who had become grandmothers clasped each others' hands while they talked.

Sunday's services at the Lanakila and Holy Name churches will never again be so well-attended, nor the choirs sing so sweetly. After church, everybody gathered on the school grounds for what should have been a rather melancholy afternoon of farewells and address exchanging.

But then Raymond Baldes brought out an ancient accordian, Gimo Souza found a guitar, and the party roared to life all over again.

—August, 1983

Shade City

Sometimes newspapers seem full of bad news. The cost of living goes up, Lahaina traffic slows down, tankers hit mines in the Persian Gulf. It can be discouraging.

Here's some good news: There is more shade in Kahului now than there used to be.

I tested this recently by walking from *The Maui News* at the Wailuku end of town to Christ the King Church at the Puunene end. It was a hot, clear morning, so I took two shirts.

Now, I've always felt that shade is a very civilized thing for a town to have. Most of Hawaii's leading towns have shade — Honolulu and Wailuku have fantastic shade, Lihue has shade, even Kona has some reputable shade, if you stay near Hulihee Palace. Hilo has world-class shade and doesn't even need it.

But until recently, Maui's thriving commercial and residential center — Kahului — has been a town without pity for the pedestrian.

To be fair, Kahului did start out as a desert, so it's had a harder row to hoe than some of Hawaii's more glamorous shade towns. It's also a new town, in business just half a lifetime. Good shade isn't built in a day.

This was clear on the first stretch of the test walk, from *The Maui News* to Kaahumanu Center. No shade. Just pitiless sun, dry grass and the hot concrete ribbon of the sidewalk. I made it to the center without hallucinating, but it was touch and go.

Staggering into the shadow of the first palm tree, I peeled off shirt No. 1, donned the second and considered my options. I could cross Kaahumanu Ave. to the MCC side, where a family lay sleeping on picnic tables in a veritable cathedral of shade. But that would involve a death-defying sprint across traffic, and my sprint had sprunt.

Also looking good was the shopping center parking lot, where healthy young monkeypods cast shade like Hawaiians throwing net. Seven sacred pools of shade stretched from Okazu-ya to Sears. But it was zigzag shade, and I wanted to go straight.

I settled on a third route — a straight shot beneath the coconut trees along the highway. It was perfect travelling shade. By walking on the shadows of the trunks, I could go from tree to tree without getting fried. It wasn't until I reached the last tree and looked back that I noticed the heavy clusters of coconuts dancing in the wind.

A diagonal course under stately monkeypods at MEO brought me to an empty lot cool with mango trees, kiawes and elephant pod trees. It was an unused place, an oasis of shade. Doves called in the high grass, and the Persian Gulf seemed far away.

The false kamanis at the Kahului Library took over next, covering me until I reached the huge mango tree behind Dairy Queen. En route I saw a man waxing his car under a tree — something that would have been impossible in Kahului 20 years ago.

From the shadow of the telephone pole near Wash House, I squinted through the bright morning light into the velvety shade of the most civilized place in town, the Kahului Shopping Center. Monkeypods planted decades ago have created a "Maui Senate" where card games and conversation flourish, sparrows hop around and people are nice to each other.

The monkeypods got me past First Interstate Bank, but then it was a long Gobi Desert past the Salvation Army store and the tempting mirage of the Kahului pool. Gasping, shirt sticking to my back, I finally reached the double row of ironwood trees that surrounds the public tennis courts.

If the old shopping center is the Parthenon of Kahului shade, the tennis courts are its Versailles. The aisle formed by the twin rows of pines is stately and geometric; the wide path a carpet of fallen needles. It seemed a fitting glade for some latter-day Louis XIV, a lazy Shade King who would yawn: "L'etat, ce n'est pa moi."

Leaving the tennis courts, I shade-hopped from mango tree to Christmas berry to banyan across an unused lot. The last leg took me across the Christ the King play field, where young poincianas were just tall enough to shade a kindergartener.

But they'll grow, just like the other shade trees planted in Kahului's brief urban history. And with luck, when that kindergartener walks across town as an adult, he won't need the second shirt.

— September, 1987

The Old Mill

In the golden light of late afternoon, the old mill looks like a ruined fortress, or a shipwreck with its prow pointing toward Haiku.

From a distance, it doesn't look like a structure at all — just a dark green hump of banyan trees surrounded by canefields.

Closer up, you realize that the "hill" beneath the trees is man-made. There are foot-thick, vine-covered walls, sagging window casements and the twisted iron girders of a roof.

Sheets of corrugated roofing iron still cling to the rafters 40 feet above what must have been a boiler room, but the rest of the roof has fallen in, forming a kind of jungle courtyard open to the sky.

Mejiro birds twitter in the banyans, and doves call softly in the stillness of this lost place. Even the light enters softly, screened by the vast canopy of foliage. In a few places, sunlight footprints the carpet of dry leaves beneath the walls, but most of the ruined building is in shadow.

While it lacks the antiquity of Angkor Wat, Nan Matol or other great ruins where a thousand monsoons have softened the works of man, the old mill has the same feeling of spent purpose and eerie repose.

It's almost as if the huge building, exhausted from turning mountains of cane into vats of molasses, weary of supporting the human community that once surrounded and depended upon it, finally caved in beneath its burden.

Reclining now in its last days, it has given itself gratefully into the green hands of nature, the planet's foremost masseuse. Tendrils of lilikoi lightly stroke the blue rock walls that trembled to the thunder of mighty engines, and muscular banyan roots knead and probe the old mill's aching foundations.

If walls could talk, what tales these could tell — of all the years and storms and engineering triumphs; of the ant lives which passed beneath this vaulted roof. No chiseled date stone remains above a fractured door, but the silence says enough: the men who built this place have gone.

In another part of the world, crowds of monkeys would shriek

144

and chatter in these treetops, and green snakes with glittering eyes would slip like liquid through the vines. Ocelets would wait in the shadowed doorways, and bristled tapirs might root and snuffle in the court.

But this is a benign ruin, home only to lizards, birds and an occasional foraging mongoose. Horses were stabled here once, but they are gone. And kolohe camp kids once "fought figs" on this forbidden battleground, but those kids have grandkids now.

So the old mill rests. The clatter of plantation tractors cultivating nearby fields brings a kind of reassurance — the work goes on — but human events are of little consequence now.

What is real is the moist caress of the Haiku wind, the toppling of root-lodged stone, the kiss of rain on upturned leaves.

— September, 1983

The big pineapple spill, Kuau. Published Sept. 7, 1976.

Big Pine Spill

It helps to be in the right place at the right time.

On Wednesday, the place was Kuau and the time was about 9:30 a.m. — shortly after the tailgate of a Kahului-bound pineapple truck fell open, spilling ripe, juicy pineapples for a full mile along Hana Highway.

By the time the driver realized what had happened and had pulled over at Kuau Store, his loss had become the public's gain.

"It's free for all!" laughed Mary Burguess, who had pulled off the road to collect some of the fruit for jelly-making. "The way they sell pineapple in the market, it's so expensive we can't buy it. So this is wonderful."

A little further up the road, Joe and Eva Solomon of Pukalani were tossing the last of several hundred smashed pineapples into the back of their pickup truck.

"It's all wasted already," Solomon reasoned happily. "So I'm going feed 'em to my cattle."

The scene was repeated from Kuau to Hookipa as delighted motorists swung their cars onto the shoulder of the road, opened their trunks, and loaded up on the sweet golden fruit.

Two lady tourists staggered past the Kuau Plaza apartments, their arms loaded with pineapples. They paused just long enough to say: "Arizona."

An Oahu woman visiting relatives here decided that Maui must indeed be no ka oi to provide free pineapples for its citizens. "All my life I've lived on Oahu," she said, "and I've never seen anything like this."

Backpacker Brian Hartwell of California didn't have a car to load his booty into, so he carried his pineapples down to the Hookipa overlook and enjoyed a Hawaiian breakfast by the sea.

Traffic in the Kahului-bound lane of the road slowed to a crawl as astonished drivers squished their way through an estimated 10,000 pounds of pineapples. Within minutes, that stretch of Hana Highway had become the sweetest, stickiest roadway in the state.

Pineapple was everywhere — chunk style, whole fruit, niblets, slices, juice and mash (mostly mash). By the time a county fire

147

truck arrived to clean up the mess, most of the undamaged fruit was long gone — but there was still plenty of work to do.

The job fell to fire captain Richard Tavares, engine operator John Rosa, fire fighter Roger Nascimento and recruit Thomas Fernandez. While policemen Robert Rapoza, Joe Vegas and William Mendes directed traffic, Tavares and Rosa walked down the road kicking pineapples onto the shoulder. Nascimento blasted water onto the road with his fire hose, and Fernandez attacked the remnants with a hoe.

It turned out to be a long road to hoe, as the job took about three hours.

The driver? After sorrowfully surveying the remains of his cargo, he climbed slowly back into the cab and drove off toward town.

— September, 1976

Wahine Bouncer

The letter bore a Makawao postmark, and it got right to the point: "To Whom It May Concern ... There's a female bouncer at Piero's Restaurant. It's the first time that we've ever seen a female bouncer working as a door lady. She handles a man like a piece of paper. The way she throws a man and lifts a man when they get out of line, it's just unbelievable. You'd think she is a man, the way she wears her cowboy hat. But when I talked to her, she is the sweetest person ... I hope that you would put it in the paper about this woman."

It's hard to ignore a letter like that.

Piero's Ristorante and Caffe sits at the corner of Makawao and Baldwin avenues, smack in the middle of Makawao town. It occupies the same rambling, tin-roofed building that housed The Tillerman before Piero's, Longhi's before The Tillerman, and Club Rodeo before Longhi's. As Maui restaurants go, it's a historic corner.

It has also been, over the years, one of Maui's rowdier corners — a place where the curious could go to find out how it feels to get slammed up against a wall or to open a beer bottle with the side of your head. Many Mauians, not being curious about such things, stayed away from that corner in droves, which made it tough to run a restaurant there.

Enter Piero Resta, a dapper Italian artist with a fondness for restaurants and a mother whose lasagna can make grown men weep.

"It's always been my vision to create a place where some of my own expression can come to life," the proprietor said one recent Saturday.

A glance around confirmed that the elements of that vision were in place. Piero's modernistic Mediterranean canvases brightened the walls. Diners dug into platters of linguini and scampi, sopping up Mama Resta's rich sauces with hunks of fresh bread. Carafes of red wine glowed in the candlelight atop linen-draped tables. The hiss of the espresso machine punctuated polite conversations.

On the bandstand, Buddy Fo's jazz-rock group "Main Course"

149

tuned up for the night's first set while prospective dancers waited at nearby tables. The bar was peopled by Makawao old-timers, California surfers, paniolos, attractive women, roguish men — all coexisting peacefully.

"What we've done here in one year, everyone is amazed," Piero beamed.

Indeed. In the past, the place was better known for chaos than cuisine. Horses were ridden through the dining room. Mirrors and windows had short lifespans. Guys in T-shirts and boots threw each other over tables.

"When we first opened, I was a nervous wreck," said Piero, terming himself more diplomat than fighter. When a patron got rowdy, he said, "I had to talk to the guy for two hours" to get him out the door. When you're managing a restaurant, two hours can take a pretty good bite out of your evening.

"I prayed every week," Piero said, "I prayed for just the right person" to come along and take that load off his shoulders.

Leilani Koa lives in Makawao with her husband Francis — a heavy equipment operator — three of their six children and four grandchildren. When not taking care of her own baby and her grandchildren, Leilani works as a "hostess" at Piero's Ristorante and Caffe.

At 39, the Oahu-born woman is no stranger to the rough and tumble of island life. Raised in Palolo Valley, she was one of nine children in a Hawaiian-Chinese family with roots in both music and law enforcement. Leilani was drawn to both, but she favored "enforcement" during her early years.

"I was a bull when I went to school," she said. "I used to fight with boys all the time. I was really a tom boy."

Her interest in contact sports later led her onto the gridiron, where she started at guard for an all-wahine football team whose finest hour was a 37-0 rout of an all-woman team from Anaheim, Calif.

"When my family heard that I was on a football team, they thought I was crazy," Leilani laughed. "They said: 'You're all guts and no brain.' When they found out I was a bouncer, they said I was really crazy."

This occurred after Leilani had spent a year studying a martial art form called "escrima," which she described as a combination of karate, kung-fu, boxing, judo and aikido. She learned to defend herself not only with her hands and feet, she said, but with weapons ranging from sickles and chako sticks to toothpicks and rolled-up newspapers.

Hearing of her prowess, the manager of a Pearl City hostess bar called "Club J" asked Leilani to become the club bouncer. Though she already had jobs playing Hawaiian music, teaching hula and working as a store detective at Parkview Gem ("One December I caught 42 shoplifters"), Leilani said the bouncership — and the $75 a night pay — appealed to her.

"It was really rough," she said. "Guys came in from Waianae and Makaha, and I had beefs all the time. If there was any trouble, I had to stop it."

Leilani stopped it for three years at Club J, including some memorable pitched battles among the Korean waitresses, before moving to Maui, her husband's home island, in 1978.

On Maui, Leilani managed a security guard firm, taught hula, played Hawaiian music with her family and brought her sixth child into the world. It was a peaceful life. Then she heard that Piero's was looking for a door person.

Three years had elapsed since her Club J days, but Leilani had stayed in shape by sparring with her husband, also a martial arts enthusiast, and working out on the 80-pound bag that hangs behind their house.

"When I first started here, it was really rough," she said, raising her voice to compete with the band. "These Makawao guys, they like to fight with the haoles. And for nothing. They figure since they're born and raised here, nobody better tell them anything."

After she had intervened in a few battles, Leilani said, word got around that a "bad wahine" was working at Piero's. "A lot of them wanted to try me because I'm a woman," she said. "They'd come up and ask me what I could do. I'd tell them: 'I'm a lover, not a fighter.'"

Humor and diplomacy will defuse most tense situations, Leilani said, and the right words in the ear or a firm hand on the shoulder will take care of all but a few of the rest. But when these techniques fail, it's nice to be able to take care of yourself.

"See this guy with the hat?" She pointed out a rangy patron who was nursing a beer at a corner table. "He used to be a bitch. Every night he'd try to pick a fight with me. He gave me a real bad time. One night I finally told him: 'If you think you can try me, Portagee, then try me, cause I'll broke you right now.'"

He tried, Leilani said, so she flipped him over a table and sent him home with a black eye. "He hasn't made any trouble since then," she said.

During the course of a Saturday night stint at Piero's, Leilani voiced what might be called the bouncer's dilemma. On the one hand, she said, "I hope there's no trouble. I hate to see trouble. That's why I always head it off if I can."

But on the other hand, she confided, "I like to mix it up, because if it's too slow you get bored. I like it when there's action. You can feel it coming."

When action does come — once or twice a week, by Leilani's estimate — she likes to get it over with as quickly as possible: "I usually just hit 'em, grab 'em by the neck, and out they go."

Speed and technique are essential in her work, since most of the men she fights are stronger than she is. Proper clothing also is important, and her usual working outfit includes — in addition to her trademark plum-colored cowboy hat — a denim jacket, roomy overalls and comfortable fighting shoes. This loose-fitting garb comes in handy when Leilani has to make a lot of moves in a hurry, as she did during one notable brawl at Club J.

"The last big fight I had, there were five guys," she said. "I couldn't do anything to stop them, so I just jumped into it." A more recent encounter, which found her under simultaneous attack by three men and a woman, was one of the few times she has had to rely on her martial arts training.

"Usually, whoever tries to hit me, I attack," she said. "But there were too many of them. So I had to flip the lady and step on her face. I really don't like to fight with the ladies, because I know what I can do to them. So I try to ignore them. I'd rather hit a man."

The opportunities to do even that have been dwindling, according to Piero's regulars. With occasional help from a mild-mannered martial artist named Leroy who rides his horse down from Kula some nights to help out ("When there's trouble in the men's room, she can't go in there," he grinned), Leilani has restored a measure of tranquility to Makawao's most famous corner.

— June, 1981

Gingerbread House

A slip of paper fluttered out of a packing box the other day like a leaf from the past.

It was a note to myself, and on it I had scribbled: "the witch," "the llama," "ice as medicine." There were also several names and something that looked like an instruction: "Just wander amiably until you hear screaming."

The notes took me back to Gingerbread House, where I worked one autumn as a day care aide watching a dozen preschoolers run amok in the gravel play yard while the real teacher led civilized activities indoors. I was allowed inside only to fix snack, mop up afterwards, clean the bathroom and set up cots for nap time. I was the Igor of Gingerbread House.

Somebody had to do it . . . and it was a learning experience.

What I learned was that things — mayhem things, usually — can happen very quickly when little kids are involved. One minute everyone is playing merrily in the sand box . . . and the next minute Alex and William are trying to pinch each other's faces off, Kayla and Whitney are having a tricycle tug-of-war, and Avery is braining Jason with a milk crate.

Five minutes later, everyone is playing merrily in the sand box again.

In the early weeks, I just wandered amiably until I heard screaming, then did what I could in the way of damage control. Ice turned out to be the best medicine, followed by bandaids.

Later I got to where I could see crises coming and defuse them by the skillful use of easels. The easels were set up under a tree, sheets of butcher paper were clipped on, and the little Picassos and O'Keefes were snapped into their smocks. Brushes and paints made from smelly powders were set out, and it was wise at that point to step back.

Brandy was my favorite artist. A 3-year-old with wild blonde curls, she would stand at her easel happily sucking a mouthful of pebbles and applying layer upon layer of black to her paper. She would surrender the pebbles on request, but I never could get her to try another color. She may have been in her "black period."

Brandy and the other painters would often produce abstracts of startling clarity and power; bold artistic statements that could have hung in New York. But they wouldn't stop there — they'd keep lashing on paint until each picture was a dark, formless swamp.

"A pumpkin!" Big Hank would announce proudly. Michelle's dark swamp would be "a doggie," while William's formless brown blob might be "me and Tony fishing." Once I left the painters alone for 14 seconds, and when I returned, three girls were carefully painting each other "witch green."

Doll play was big, and the favorite was "the witch," a nondescript blonde doll who looked nothing whatsoever like a witch. But she had gained that title by consensus, and she was always taken first at nap time. I have no idea why.

The biggest event of the week was "the garbage truck!" whose Tuesday morning approach would send Big Hank into a spasm of euphoria and terror. Crazed with anticipation, he would race around the yard shouting until I could get the kids in line and out the gate to the street. There we would cower against a plank fence until the thundering machine with its giant retractable arm had eaten all the garbage in the neighborhood. The driver always waved as he drove off.

Other adult heroes were Fernando and his crew of yardmen, who came every few weeks to trim hedges and dazzle the kids with their leaf - blowers. And once a husband - wife team showed up at Gingerbread House with a llama they were using to hype children's aspirin. The llama looked warily through his great liquid eyes at the advancing line of gnomes, but the kids were spooked enough to be gentle.

Halloween was spooky, too, until the kids realized that a costume didn't permanently change you. William was the test. His mother had made him a wonderful cow costume, but when the cow head was lowered over William's, everyone fell silent with fear and wonder.

Finally William's best friend, Tony, stepped bravely up to the cow and gazed into the eye holes.

"William," he said, his voice quavery. "Are you in there?"

There was no reply, because William himself wasn't sure.

— *September, 1987*

Holy Ghost Feast

A fresh plumeria lei circled the marble shoulders of a small headstone behind Holy Ghost Church. "Our son Joseph E. Martin," the inscription read, listing dates that were too close together.

Other small headstones dotted the grassy slope that rises from the church to the statue of the Blessed Virgin. Bright sprays of daffodils, red carnations and purple heather glowed in the hazy morning sunshine. Flowers for the flowers of Kula who bloomed too briefly.

Voices rose from the church below and floated like sunshine over the small cemetery, singing the mass in Portuguese, as it has been sung for generations. The air was still and cool. In the distance below, islands rose from a flat blue sea.

It was the day of the Holy Ghost Feast, a day of celebration and remembrance, of penitence and merrymaking. A day when the circle of life is completed for the living and the dead.

Inside the vaulted church, Father Paul Zegers placed his hands on the red-draped altar. "The Church is the person of Christ among us," he said. And indeed, a gentle presence seemed to walk among the parishioners that day.

The people rose from the pews and filed into the sunlit churchyard where food and game booths were being readied for the village fair ahead. Young hogs and fattened cattle snuffled in their holding pens, awaiting the afternoon livestock auction.

Soon the acolytes emerged from the eight-sided church, followed by Father Paul and pretty Roberta Goble, who would represent Queen Isabella of Portugal in the traditional procession of the crown. A column of children dressed as angels, saints and prophets tagged behind like the bright tail of a kite.

The silver crown that Goble bore on a velvet cushion as she and her train slowly circled the church grounds has great significance for the Catholic people of Kula. It symbolizes a 600-year-old event: Queen Isabella of Portugal's gift of her eight-sided crown to the Church of the Holy Ghost in Lisbon, a city then withering from drought.

In so asserting her faith, that 14th century monarch struck a chord that resonates to this day among the Catholics whose grandparents and great-grandparents built their homes and farms and lives on the drought-parched slopes of Haleakala.

When those early settlers raised their church at Waiakoa in the 1890s, they gave it eight sides, topped it with a crown-like steeple and named it Holy Ghost Church. And in good times and bad, they and their descendants have for more than 90 years commemorated Queen Isabella's act of generosity.

For if anything characterizes the annual Holy Ghost Feast, it is generosity. Cattle and pigs and chickens, produce and baked goods, even the prizes for the game booths do not have to be bought. They are donated. The scores of people who bake the bread, crochet the prizes, work in the booths, slaughter the livestock, cook the feast and clean up afterwards do not have to be paid. Theirs is a labor of love for the church.

And each year the church returns that bounty during the Feast of the Holy Ghost. There is no charge for the traditional Sunday supper of poi, laulau and sweet potato that each year feeds thousands of parishioners and guests. The scale of that meal alone is staggering — 15,500 laulaus were prepared for this year's feast.

Such fees as were charged for the skill games, the food and produce booths and the Saturday night dance seemed absurdly modest in this high-priced Year of Our Lord 1982. Carnival "scrips" sold for 10 cents, and a handful of those went a long way. Seven got you a savory cup of chow fun; seven more an ear of Kula sweet corn. For 10 scrips, you could get eight still-steaming malasadas, and for 15 you could have all the teriyaki you thought you could eat.

There was generosity of another sort as well. After the symbolic crown had been placed among the anthuriums of the temporary shrine, after the Instamatics had finished clicking and the television cameras had moved off, silent parishioners stepped up to the shrine and solemnly tucked money into the crown. For some, it was a great deal of money.

Its critics say that the Catholic Church takes more than it returns; that it rides the backs of the world's poor like a heavy horseman. But at Waiakoa the church seems the horse, not the rider. It carries its people through the generations, through times of poverty and times of plenty. It is the living heart at the center of their lives.

There is a mystery about the Holy Ghost Feast: How can so few feed and entertain so many, decade after decade? It isn't done for money, prestige or power. It must be done for love, in the spirit of generosity.

That spirit rang out in Sam Fevella's voice as he auctioned off loaves of bread, animals and sweet cakes. It sparkled in Cecilia Ventura's eyes as she gave out handmade prizes in the penny-plunk booth. It flashed in George Ventura's grin as he coordinated the massive parish hall feast, and it guided the hands of Daniel and

Nancy Purdy as they squeezed out cup after cup of poi.

Drucilla Castro, Mary Aruda and Rose Medeiros expressed it in the underpriced handmade finery for sale in their booth, as did Marilyn Fernandez and Cindy Freitas at their country store. Vivian, Lovey and Jo Gregulho didn't grumble when the malasadas spat hot oil, and Frank Molina stirred his wok of chow fun with a smile on his face.

And when the feast was over, the carnival and auction finished for another year, when the Brittains and Tavareses and DePontes and Boteilhos and Otanis and Pimentels had all gone home, the spirit of love remained, resting gently as a plumeria lei on the marble shoulders of a small boy's grave.

—June, 1982

Maalaea
Freight Train

While the Pentagon weapons scandal rocked Washington last week and the worst drought in 50 years withered the Midwest, Maui's first big summer swell drew hundreds of surfers to the island's leeward shores.

There are times — many times, actually — when this corner must set down the burden of commenting on weighty national and international affairs to answer a higher call: "Surf's Up!" Last week was one of those times.

(Non-surfers, parents and employers of surfers, and anyone else who has ever had to listen to a surfer describe a "totally awesome, infinite, unreal tube ride" should turn the page here, dude.)

So there I was — white above me, white behind me, streaking across a 6-foot face at Sea Flites, totally blinded by spray, the tube grinding closer and closer. Then the backwash hit . . . Ba-Whoom! Airbone, brah!

Even more than the big blue swells that hammer Maui's windward coasts all winter, a meaty south swell can depopulate job sites, postpone yard work, cripple commerce and industry, and leave angry brides fuming alone at altars. (Well, maybe not — but check the groom's hair for salt.)

The south swell is a sleeper here. Girdled by other islands, Maui's leeward side misses many of the summer swells that peel off for weeks on end at places like Kona, Ala Moana and Poipu. Of our spots, Lahaina usually gets the most action — overhead at the harbor, Shark Pit and Mala Wharf; tapering off at Olowalu and Thousand Peaks.

But every so often, storm waves generated far below the equator crank through the channel between Kahoolawe and Lanai, and Maalaea Bay becomes a wind-lashed caldron of surge and spray. There are bigger, prettier summer spots — but none quite as dramatic as Maalaea.

Trade winds howling through the saddle blast the incoming sets head-on, stiffening the waves and standing them up, like a linebacker driving into a running back. The waves steam and buck like horses, and the air fills with stinging manes of spray.

At Maalaea Harbor, these photogenic effects are heightened by a monster "backwash" that races seaward after each wave belts the wall. Raking the incoming wave at a wicked angle, the backwash turns each new peak into a rippling fan of water, a doo-wop spirtcurl for Nalu.

The result is spectacular for viewers and quasi-religious for surfers, especially those courageous enough to ride the Maalaea "Freight Train" on a big day. This huge, hollow right is the Wabash Cannonball of waves, barreling a quarter-mile from the harbor entrance toward the condos on the beach.

The train analogy is apt not only for the wave's size and speed, but also for what happens to you when you fall off. There are other spots that test the surfer's will to live — the big left at Paukukalo is no picnic, and a close-out day at Hookipa can certainly exercise the heart — but few administer such a thorough, professional beating as a 10-wave set at Freight Train.

When it gets big out there, I just watch. The first time I saw that place really crank was in 1974, when there were still houses on the beach and the Coast Guard hadn't cinder-blocked the view from Jimmy Uno's store. I had just moved to Maui from Guam and was prowling for surf in my rusty Datsun pickup.

"Forget it," a co-worker told me. "There's no surf on Maui in the summer. Lanai and Kahoolawe block all the waves."

I took a spin along the south shore anyway. The first thing I remember seeing as I drove down from Waikapu was a long line of spray visible over the cane tops. From McGregor Point to The Dump at Cape Kinau, the whole bay was whitewater. It seemed like there was a new break every few hundred yards.

I watched Freight Train flatten a few brave surfers and one guy on a paipo board. It was an easy 10 feet that day, breaking into a 20-knot wind way out past the end of the wall. The waves hissed and thundered past like those huge sand worms in "Dune." I haven't seen Maalaea that big since.

Yet guys were out there — and every 20 minutes or so, somebody would be in the right place for the right wave and make it all the way across. We cowards on the breakwall cheered and whistled . . . and stayed right where we were.

— June, 1988

Pier One Duck

He is afraid.

He is totally alone.

He is 3,000 miles from home.

But he's not "E.T. the Extraterrestrial;" he's Ernie, the Pier One Duck. And, well, he's not "totally" alone — there are a few sparrows hopping around nearby. But there aren't any other ducks on Pier One.

You see, Ernie is a "stowaway" duck. The people in the Matson office at Pier One aren't really sure how he got here, but they think he waddled off a barge that came to Kahului Harbor from Seattle a couple of weeks ago.

Not that Maui's such a bad place for a duck. The Matson folks feed Ernie bread and rice every morning, and he gets to watch the crew of the tugboat "Joe Sevier" hose down the decks.

But it's not really home. The drizzly marshes of Seattle — and the winsome lady ducks who wade and quack there — are 3,000 miles away. Ernie seems to realize this. According to the Matson employees, he "disappears" at about 9:30 every morning and doesn't come back until nightfall.

"I think he flies over to the breakwater side and stays over there during the day," one man said.

But what does he do on that lonely breakwater? Does he stare wistfully out to the eastern horizon, thinking of his marshy home and the girlfriend duck he left behind? Or is he glad to be away from all that — perhaps a fugitive from the law in some other jurisducktion?

We'll probably never know, because Ernie doesn't quack much about his past. He just pads silently along the wharf, pausing now and then to drink from a puddle of rainwater or eat the middle out of a slice of bread. (He doesn't eat his crusts; hence the sparrows that follow him around.)

All we know for sure is that Ernie is a large brown duck with a white throat and belly and a few emerald green feathers on his wings and back. And, if he lays some eggs, we know he'll need a different name. But for now, Ernie is a mystery duck, the latest in a long line of handsome rogues who have stowed away on seagoing vessels to "jump ship" at some exotic port.

Like other soldiers of fortune before him, he may find the island to his liking, settle down, marry some pretty Maui mallard and raise a brood of little Ernies and Ernestines.

But judging from the restless look in his eye and the proud tilt of his bill, Ernie may be a bird of another feather . . . a dyed-in-the-down adventurer for whom Maui is just another landfall on the long stowaway voyage of life.

— August, 1982

Putting ice to the catch, aku boat Orion. Published June 29, 1981.

A is for Aku

It's past one in the morning at Maalaea, and the only sounds in this sleeping harbor are the chink of halyards against aluminum masts and the gentle slap and creak of boats at their moorings.

It's a warm, still night, the air scented with kiawe blossoms. A good night to walk past the darkened shapes of fishing boats — Cutty Sark, Bluemax, Bobbie T., Lady of Fatima, Cadi IV, V Sisters, Reel Hooker. The old and new: wooden sampans of all sizes, some built in back yards long ago; modern fiberglass charter boats with tuna towers and television. All dark and silent.

Then a starter motor kicks over, and the drumming of a big diesel can be heard down past Jimmy Uno's store. In the eerie glow of floodlights, barefoot men move swiftly over the deck of a large sampan, opening hatches, stowing provisions, casting off lines. The aku boat Orion is putting to sea.

At half past one, as he has done nearly every night for the past 35 years, Captain Hajime Hamashige signals for the stern line to be let go. With a touch of the throttle, he eases the 85-foot, 25-ton vessel away from the dock.

For the next 18 hours, Hamashige and his men will pursue flocks of seabirds and the schools of skipjack tuna beneath them. The chase will take them around Maui and 15 miles out to sea. The sun will be hellishly hot; the ocean calm and darkest blue. When the Orion glides into Kahului Harbor at dusk, its hold will contain the plump silver bodies of a couple of hundred "small aku" — not quite enough to cover the cost of the trip. The fishermen will take home a few fish, but no pay.

It's a hard way to make a living.

A golden crescent moon pokes through the clouds as the big sampan clears Maalaea Harbor, and galaxies of lights and stars twinkle in the blackness astern. But the men of the Orion are too busy for sightseeing. While most stow their belongings, two men strip, don goggles, and lower themselves into lighted baitwells shimmering with thousands of "iao" netted in the shallows off Ukumehame the previous day.

Mallets in hand, the men pound fitted wooden blocks into the drainage holes at the bottom of the baitwells to prevent the silver-green minnows from returning to the Pacific prematurely. The tiny baitfish are the key to the success or failure of the voyage. They will be used later in the day to lure schools of aku close enough to the Orion's stern to be hooked by the fishermen and flung into the boat.

The aku — and the fishermen — prefer a baitfish called "nehu," but the nehu are not abundant this year, so iao it must be. 'As why hard.

Built on Oahu in 1947, the Orion is one of a dwindling fleet of "classic" Hawaiian sampans launched before aluminum, fiberglass and television went to sea. Her lines come, centuries old, from Japan — the high, narrow prow with its faceted anchor stay, a red star, and the name Orion pounded into the thick wood with mallet and chisel.

Beneath the gracefully sloping foredeck, piled with nets, floats, anchors and coiled line, there is a berth with four bunks for the crew. The solid, square cabin juts up amidships, surmounted by whip antennas and tall enough for the captain and his spotters to command a sweeping view of the horizon through its many windows. It contains, in addition to the ship's wheel, compass, barometer and throttles, six more bunks for the crew's periodic naps. Mounted above the wheel is a tiny wooden replica of a Buddhist shrine, its miniature doors swung open to reveal the ancient, graceful kanji of the omamori, or fisherman's prayer.

Beneath the cabin is the engine room, home of the 450-horsepower marine diesel that keeps the Orion cruising at 12 knots through heavy seas or doldrums. Next to it is the cramped galley, where some of the best meals in Hawaii are prepared daily. Astern are the baitboxes, ice holds and the low-lying fantail, where the fishermen will maintain a precarious foothold while slinging thrashing aku bodies over their shoulders with short bamboo poles. The lavatory is a single bollard mounted onto the stern with a short loop of rope attached.

The smell of burning tires indicates that the Orion is passing Olowalu Dump. All is quiet on deck, the eight-man regular crew having retired to various bunks to catch a couple of hours of sleep before the sampan nears its first objective — a state "fishing buoy" off Huelo.

In addition to its regular crew, who share the proceeds (and costs) of each trip, the Orion today carries 11 "guests," some of whom are now sacked out on the deck, their heads supported by small wooden blocks. The guests range in age from 12-year-old

Manuel Santiago, the boat's rascally "mascot," to 61-year-old Hiro Nakagawa, a retired contractor and a veteran of 45 years on aku boats.

By the time the Orion has rounded Kapalua and passed the beacon at Nakalele Point, breakfast cook Larry Mandawe has lit the gas burners in the tiny galley, taken the pans from their hooks on the bulkhead, and is slicing green onions and Portuguese sausage on a cutting board.

Soon Farmer John links, eggs, rice, onions and fillets of aku in shoyu - sugar sauce are sizzling in the hot black pans. The fragrances awaken guest engineer Livian "Sonny" Bal, a friendly, growly bear of a man who had been dozing in the warmest spot on the ship, the doorway to the engine room. He grumbles and goes below to check the generator.

Meanwhile, Mandawe cooks while the Orion plunges through the pre-dawn darkness. Wearing only a pair of shorts, he deftly slices, dices and stir-fries various ingredients, his bare feet flanked by pots of hot coffee and tea, his bare midriff just inches from the flaming burners. Rocking with the swells, working in the glare of a naked 60-watt bulb, a cigarette dangling from the corner of his mouth, he fixes breakfast for 19 men. Nothing gets burned, nothing is wasted, and the meal is served hot.

The food, laid out on the planks of the afterdeck and eaten with chopsticks from bowls, vanishes in eight minutes. The implements are washed and put away in half that time.

By first light, the crew and guests have risen from their short naps, eaten breakfast and washed up, and now prepare their poles and hooks for the long day of fishing ahead. Each man readies several poles — short bamboo staves in case a huge school hits at once; longer poles if the aku are fewer in number; double poles in the event the Orion is lucky enough to encounter a school of otari or "big aku."

While it is still a couple of months before the peak otari season, these 20- to 35-pound aku are preferred over the five-pound "small aku" usually caught in June. The big aku, which may take two men to boat, keep better and stay "red" longer — an important marketing factor, since much of an otari catch can be sold at premium prices for sashimi. Small aku, which loses its color more quickly, usually ends up as canned tuna.

While the others are readying their gear below, Capt. Hamashige stands in the wheelhouse with Hakaru "Gombe" Ibara and Larry Mandawe. The three men scan the lightening horizon for the flocks of birds that indicate the presence of baitfish and tuna. Holding heavy binoculars to their eyes, the three rock slowly forward and back as the Orion rides over the swells, rarely lowering their glasses. The captain pauses from time to time to turn the steering wheel a degree or two.

Hamashige and his spotters will stand like this for the next 10 hours.

"Otari! Otari!"
"Throw bait! Feed some bait!"
"Come, come, come, big aku! Coming down the side, now, now!"
"Yah! Yah! Yah!"

A big aku has hit one of two lures that the Orion trolls, and the sight of its flashing, torpedo-shaped body throws the fishermen into a frenzy. Hamashige cuts the engines, the men fall silent, and suddenly the only sounds are the lonely, eerie cry of seabirds and the whacking of bamboo poles on the ocean.

A water spray is activated to excite whatever fish may be feeding in the area, and first mate Masato Yoshino adroitly flips baitfish from one of the wells into the ocean alongside the Orion. They enter the water with a silver flash like a handful of flung coins, but the big aku have better things to eat than iao. Only one fish is boated. The water spray is turned off, the poles put down, and the Orion plunges onward.

With little variation, this pattern is repeated to no avail for the rest of the morning. Finally, at about noon, the Orion reaches an area of boiling water.

"This one might bring some action," Ibara says. He's right. Soon the deck is alive with the flapping, whapping, five-pound bodies of small aku, and the men at the stern are steadily heaving more over their shoulders. The fish rain through the air for about five minutes, and then the action stops as suddenly as it started. The school has sounded.

The men don't know it at the time, but this will be their catch for the day — about 1,500 to 2,000 pounds of fish. A good catch for 1981 might be 20,000 pounds. Oldtimers like Hiro Nakagawa remember days when 40,000 pounds of fish was boated — 30,000 pounds from a single school.

After several more hours of chasing, much fruitless flogging, baiting and spraying of the ocean, and no further catches, Hamashige orders his crew to "Ice 'em up," and the Orion heads for faraway Kahului Harbor with its meager catch.

A great deal of work remains before the crew can rest. One of the baitboxes is drained, the aku are gathered and loaded into it, and huge blocks of ice are shattered over the fish. Poles and hooks are stowed, the blood-stained decks are scrubbed, and the men then strip down and scrub themselves and their clothes, hanging the latter on lines attached to the cabin before changing. At last there is time for a smoke and a nap.

On the Orion this day are regular crew members Captain Hajime Hamashige, first mate Masato Yoshino, and fishermen Charles Cramer, John Kaauwai, Larry Mandawe, Masa Yatomi, Gary Ibara and Abner Brown. Guests are Hiro Nakagawa, Sonny Bal, Aku Takitani, Hakaru Ibara, Butch Graham, Buster Young, Hiromi Fujimura, Ron Tomishima, Manuel Santiago and Myles Murata.

—June, 1981

Sea-A-Rama

"Galveston, O Galveston . . . I can hear your sea waves crashing . . . ."

I always disliked that song. I don't know if it had to do with Glen Campbell's adenoidal whine or the song's plodding lyrics, but "Galveston" never cracked the Top 40 on my hit parade.

The song that was big in Galveston the summer I lived there was "Bare Footin'," a spunky hit at The Beach Hut and other beer joints where college kids danced the Shag on the island's Gulf Coast.

My roomies and I clattered out to The Beach Hut astride a coal black, 1948 Harley Davidson three-wheeler. The bike was in its dotage, but to us it was baaaad. It had a hand shifter and a "meter maid" box from which young lunatics could scan the horizon for girls. You do a lot of that at 19.

Larry and Victor were brothers from Waco — a hardscrabble mid-Texas city so nondescript it made Galveston look like Paris. In the summer of 1966, we three worked at Sea-A-Rama, a new marine park on the island's marshy west end.

Sea-A-Rama was not a world-class attraction. Its big draws were a porpoise show run by a pair of West Texas oil riggers and an aquarium whose Ovaltine-colored waters hid several "gars" — huge, torpid fish that moped in the tank like patients in a dentist's waiting room.

I had gone to Galveston hoping to land a glamorous job as a porpoise trainer at Sea-A-Rama, but I wound up digging ditches for $1.25 an hour, cursing the 95-degree heat and breaking rocks on the marine park's chain gang. In addition to Larry and Victor, this outfit included several men from southern Louisiana. It took me a while to figure out their curious, sing-song dialect.

"Toe-wum, Toe-wum," my co-worker Samson Jones sang the first day. "Whayeeze dee woe-duh kay-un?"

I'd heard a lot of dialects as a kid in Hawaii, but deep Louisianese wasn't one of them. After several repetitions of the question, I finally just said: "Hmmm, that's right," leaving Samson to find the water can himself.

Samson Jones was the first person I'd ever met who sported a gold-capped tooth with a star cut out. He was 50, invariably cheerful, and built like a young bull. He told me he had left his 15-year-old bride in Natchitoches and had driven his truck to Galveston to find work. I think that's what he said.

Interpreting Larry and Victor's twangy Waco drawl was a little easier, but some of their expressions startled me. For instance, when Victor was preparing to spit — always a riveting performance — Larry would chuckle: "Look out, Vic's gonna hawk an oyster."

The brothers and I shared a weatherbeaten, two-story house which leaned drunkenly toward the murky bait ponds at its feet. This pronounced "list" gave the house a doomed, nautical feel, like the final hours of the Titanic.

The up side was that dropped objects always rolled to the low edge of the living room, which made for easy retrieval. Not that we had a lot of objects to retrieve. At $1.25 an hour, we lived pretty close to the bone.

We were the first people in 15 years to live in that decrepit shanty, so we started from scratch. We hammered "furniture" together out of crates and scrap lumber we found under the house. It wasn't The Alexander Collection, but it held our weight.

We found that by beveling the legs, we could make the furniture list in the opposite direction from the house, so that when we sat in it, we were nearly level. This is the kind of thing colleges don't teach.

They also don't teach you how to forage for food. The brothers and I were so broke that summer that we became expert seiners, dragging the nearby ponds for freshwater crabs that would go into a cook pot along with a packet of "Crab Broil."

Watermelons, corn flakes, wild tomatoes and "gumdrop cookies" — the latter mailed in coffee tins by Vic and Larry's worried mother — rounded out our diet. When these gave out, we would play peek-a-boo with toddlers in family restaurants. The rapt toddlers would forget to eat, the families would leave, and Larry, Vic and I would swoop down on the kids' plates.

Nowdays, my displeasure at hearing "Galveston, O Galveston" is dispelled by the loopy memories that song conjures up.

—June, 1988

Windsurfers

Something special happens to Maui's north shore in October. The season's first rains have scrubbed the land and the air. The ballfields at Baldwin and Paia parks are as green as pool tables. Hibiscus blossoms flame from roadside hedges.

Offshore, majestic blue swells peel across the outer reefs and sweep into the bays, dazzling the eye with foam. Stately squalls proceed up the coast from Hana like retainers to some ancient queen, trailing velvet holokus of rain. They pass, and the azure October sky brightens once again.

The sun is lower now in the sky than in summer. Its soft light streams in at an angle, saturating the land and sea with color, painting the flanks of Haleakala rose red by late afternoon.

Nowhere are the colors more intense these days than along the white-capped coastline from Kanaha to Hookipa. There, hot pinks and lime greens catch the eye; reds and yellows and purples dart across the cobalt sea.

They are the sails of windsurfers. Seen from land, they look like seagoing butterflies or creatures from a fantasy — swift and graceful and exotic. They seem to skim across the water effortlessly, as though propelled by the autumn sun itself.

But appearances can be deceiving, as anyone who has spent 45 minutes falling off a windsurf board will attest. The sport requires strength, agility and stamina; the reflexes of a gymnast and the patience of a saint.

At its best, it combines the arts of wave riding, sailing, ski jumping and even deep sea fishing — some windsurfers troll for papio and come in with dinner for 12. And eventually, each windsurfer becomes a meteorologist, alert to every nuance of the wind, every boil of the cloudscape.

When the sport first hit, the occasional car top stacked with boards, booms and canvas sailbags drew curious stares, and there was a stirring of resentment from surfers concerned that the faster craft would crowd them out of the breaks.

Both sports are exciting to watch. The surfers ride tight up against the curling waves, timing their turns and drawing lines of

170

acceleration across the steep faces that will put them into the "blue room," the silent, revolving cylinder where time melts like a Dali watch.

Judgment gets you there, and speed keeps you there, but it is the speed of the wave. Windsurfing adds another dimension — the speed and maneuverability of sail. No longer confined to the curl, windsurfers range across the entire breadth and duration of the wave, riding from its infancy beyond the reef to its whispered parting on the sand.

In between, they cut similar acceleration lines, but faster and cleaner than the sail-less surfboards. Where a turn in surfing is a calculated debt to the wave — which can be a very heavy collection agency at times — the windsurfers seem almost heedless of the wave's force. Gripping the wind with their arms and backs, pumping off the ocean with their legs, they fly across the waves, turn with sweeping grace and power, then lean back against a hissing trampoline of wind and toppling water.

It's not supposed to be. But man wasn't supposed to hang and bank on the thermals, either, or descend to places where the carcasses of ships long dead surrender to that jewelled necromancer, the sea. Man wasn't supposed to go to the moon, or forward through time.

If the great time traveler Leonardo lived today, he would laugh and clap his hands to see the windsurfers . . . before retiring to his study to figure out how to free them from gravity entirely, or how best to use them in some amphibious landing against the Borgias' enemies.

And if Cyrano could see the windsurfers, he might rub his nose and rethink his plan to reach the moon with helium balloons and a flock of geese. Why not windsurf to the moon? With silken sails trimmed to the interstellar wind, the great lover is pulled moonward on beams of silver light. Allons!

But windsurfing belongs to our time. It is the child of 20th century engineering, space-age alloys, better living through chemistry. Yet there is something else, something Leonardo and Cyrano would understand — the power to dream the future.

Windsurfing says: Now we can do this . . . what else is possible?

— October, 1983

Honolua Store operator Shoon Tet Hew. Published Aug. 16, 1983.

Honolua Store

In her precise bookkeeper's hand, Henrietta Mahuna enters columns of figures in a bound ledger. Except for the country-western lament issuing from the portable tape player at her elbow, the back room of Honolua Store is as quiet as dust.

Arrows of afternoon sunlight glance off empty cardboard boxes stacked near the rear screen door, and a light breeze rustles sheets of plastic draped over empty display counters. Two sacks of Maui onions share a storage bin with a pile of unsold zoris.

At the other end of the long, high-ceilinged room, the kitchen is cool and dark. The day's 105 plate lunches have been prepared and sold, the cook pots scoured, the woks hung back up on the wall. On a shelf in the pantry, among the cans of bamboo shoots, Chili Laredo and chicken soup base, a gallon tin without a label has been hand-lettered "corned pipi."

Through a screen door between the kitchen and the front office, proprietor Shoon Tet Hew can be seen composing an ad for the following week's editions of *The Maui News.*

"For sale: chill boxes, freezer boxes, antique safe (1,000 pounds), book cases, tables, adding machine, cash register, walk-in chiller, miscellaneous merchandise. Must be sold by Aug. 31, 1983. All sales final."

After 65 years of business, Honolua Store will close at the end of this month. No longer the hub of a major plantation town, the rambling old structure is now an island of history in the middle of a jet-set resort.

The wooden planks of its floors, worn smooth by generations of work boots, now show the spike marks of tasseled golf shoes. The ceiling that protected racks of clothes, sacks of rice and chicken feed, kerosene stoves, rolls of yardage, garden tools, dry goods and housewares, school supplies, shoes, fishing tackle, fresh meat and produce for a vanished community now sags with weariness.

But the store — or at least the location of the store — remains valuable. It borders a tree-lined road that is to become the new gateway to the Kapalua resort. The store or whatever replaces it will be one of the first things Kapalua residents and guests will see.

Hew isn't sure what will become of the building he has leased for the past 22 years. He has heard that Maui Land and Pine may fix up the store and reopen it as something else, but that's no concern of his. At 72, he is ready to retire.

A voice from the front of the store calls "Gas, Mr. Hew." The stoop-shouldered storekeeper rises from his desk and walks slowly past the shelves of snack foods, cartons of beer and beach toys that have become his stock in trade in recent years.

Pausing for a moment at the wide store entrance, he gazes out over a scene he has come to know well: a manicured fairway, a road bordered by stately Norfolk pines, the misty shape of Molokai across the white-capped channel.

A golf cart whirs past the store, and Hew walks down the front steps to pump gas for a workman with four ripe pineapples in the bed of his pickup truck. Other trucks are parked in the shade of a nearby monkeypod tree, where their burly drivers pau hana the afternoon away with a couple of cold 12-packs.

Wiping his hands on a rag, Hew climbs slowly back up the front steps onto the shaded porch. An elderly Filipino man sits on a bench beneath a peeling "Pepsi" decal, sipping a can of soda and watching four smartly dressed golfers smack drives from the third tee.

A group of laughing tourists emerges from the store and sits on the other bench to eat hot dogs, candy and ice cream bars. The feet in their new zoris are sunburned and speckled with sand. The father and his two sons wear matching "Kapalua" t-shirts on which butterflies emerge from pineapples.

At the cash register, longtime employee Orpha Kaina rings up a purchase for a couple of surfers, then indicates an old metal receipt machine that records in triplicate the orders of "charge" customers.

"Mr. Hew still carries charges," she says proudly. "He's one of the last ones."

Rummaging in a display counter whose glass doors are filmed with dust, she produces a yellowed cardboard packet of brass-plated "paper fasteners," a box of fountain pen points and a booklet of blank receipt forms labeled "Baldwin Packers, Honolua Store, 1940."

A nearby table displays sale items from a more recent but still bygone era: spools of Beldon-Corticelli mercerized cotton thread, hand-sewn canvas fishing tabis, tins of "Baitbits" rat-killer, a pile of Taihei "super eye glass" snorkeling goggles and several "Dazey Foot Saver" units ("After a long day of work or play, treat yourself to a soothing, vibrating massage, wet or dry.").

Overhead, atop tall cabinets mounted along two walls of the room, giant cardboard cigarette boxes march in place, a nicotine army passing in review. When it is time to take them down, Henrietta Mahuna's husband Solomon or Hew's niece, Diana Akiona, will climb an antique wheeled ladder that rolls along a track attached to the ceiling.

"This is one of the old kind," Henrietta says of the ladder. "You won't find them like this any more. Everybody wants to buy it, but Mr. Hew won't sell it, because it goes back to the owner."

Back at her desk in the cavernous storeroom, she recalls the time she and her helpers made and sold 489 plate lunches in a single day, mostly to construction workers then building Kapalua and other nearby resorts.

"It was just like a carnival, those days," she chuckles. "Workers coming back and forth, golfers coming back and forth. We've even had people coming all the way from Wailuku for the lunches."

Returning to her work, she enters the day's plate lunch sales in the bound ledger. Only two more weeks to go. Then the lunches, the ledger and her 20-year job will be history. Except for the country-western music playing on the tape machine, the back room of Honolua Store is as quiet as dust.

— August, 1983

Christmas
Close to Nature

Sitting in a guava tree in the darkness in the pouring rain, Richard Ferenzak and Mike Carroll imagined how the other people in the world were spending Christmas Eve.

"I thought of a family in the Midwest sitting around a blazing fire," Ferenzak said.

"I just thought of a blazing fire," Carroll said.

Actually, the two shivering Maui men had been enjoying a fire of their own just hours earlier, but it had gone out when the Iao River rose six feet in 15 minutes and engulfed the little island where they had pitched camp.

"You usually hear it called Iao Stream," Ferenzak said. "But it became a raging river, with rapids and waterfalls and whole trees washing down it. I've seen whitewater in other rivers, but I'd never seen anything like this."

How did two normal, healthy, seemingly sane individuals end up spending Christmas Eve in a guava tree and Christmas Day fighting for their lives in the rapids?

"The idea was to spend Christmas close to nature," said the 34-year-old Ferenzak, the Maui manager for a solar heating firm. "We thought it would be nice to get away from the pressures of business, just camp out and look at the stars. We didn't have any intention of getting that heavy into it."

What they got into was a 40-hour ordeal that pushed both men to the limits of their wit and endurance, claimed their dog and most of their gear, and taught them "a lot in a very short period of time," as Ferenzak put it.

Here's roughly how it went:

Carroll, 30, a lifelong Hawaii resident and experienced West Maui hiker, and his house-mate Ferenzak, a 13-year Maui resident with considerable backpacking and mountaineering experience, wanted to hike through Iao Valley and come out Olowalu Valley. In addition, Carroll wanted to be the first person he knew to make the trip with a dog, so he brought his brown-and-white pit bull "E.T." along.

When they set out from their rented house on Iao Road at about

176

1 p.m. Christmas Eve, the two also carried packs, enough trail mix and crackers for two days, sleeping bags, hammocks, rain tarps, cameras, a copy of *Hiking Maui*, a good topographical map of the West Maui Mountains, two waterproof flashlights, a knife and a 100-foot length of rope.

"Our plan was just to get into the valley a little ways Saturday and make camp so we'd have an early start for Olowalu on Sunday," Ferenzak said. "We had checked with the weather service an hour before we left, and they said: 'Partly cloudy, maybe some showers.'"

"I had checked the satellite weather map and seen the low pressure area off Kauai," Carroll added, "but it looked like it was going to move off to the northeast. The four days before had been beautiful, and we figured our timing was perfect."

Their timing was perfect for the heaviest rainstorm of the year, a Christmas Day deluge that dumped 8 inches of water on Wailuku and brought the rest of the island to a standstill. But back to the story.

Rock-hopping up Iao Stream Saturday afternoon, Ferenzak, Carroll and E.T. reached the major fork at the rear of the valley and headed up the left stream, where the hiking book indicated that the trail to Olowalu took off along a rockslide above a waterfall and fern grotto.

"It was so overgrown we missed it completely," Ferenzak said of the Olowalu cutoff. "We went on about three more miles until we reached an island with bananas and guava trees growing out of it. That's where we decided to camp."

Their topo map indicated that the island where they stopped was "right next to the little red square that says: 'wettest spot on Earth,'" Carroll said, but conditions were ideal when the hikers strung their hammocks at dusk on Saturday.

"It was great," Carroll said. "We had a regular little campsite, with the dog sleeping next to the fire and the hammocks hung in the guava trees. It was a beautiful night — warm, no wind, calm — it seemed perfect."

"Then it started to rain," Ferenzak said.

By midnight, the rain was falling "pretty hard," and soon the hikers noticed alarming changes in the "trickle of a stream" that had separated their island from the steep ravines on either side.

"All of a sudden the river rose up, covered the campfire and went underneath our hammocks," Ferenzak said. "Then it went down as suddenly as it came up. But by the time it receded, the 'little trickle' was above our knees."

Ferenzak, a New Jesey native who learned his mountaineering skills in Wyoming and the Colorado Rockies, decided it was time to take some precautionary measures. He tied the 100-foot line to a guava tree on the island, looped it around another tree across the stream, then tied it off to a third tree 20 feet up the steep stream bank.

"Richard was a regular little busy bee," Carroll laughed, "but I wasn't worried. I just lay in my hammock and tried to stay dry."

By 3 a.m. it was obvious that they could forget about staying dry or staying on the island, for that matter.

"There were still a few dry spots on the island," Carroll said, "but the water between the island and the bank was already chest high and going about 40 miles an hour. We looked at it with our flashlights, and all we could see was muddy rapids."

Pulling themselves hand-over-hand along the safety line, they managed at length to get themselves and their packs up into the branches of the guava tree on the far stream bank, but there was no hope for E.T.

"The stream had been rising continuously, and it was roaring so loud we couldn't hear each other," Ferenzak said. "If you lost your footing, you were gone."

"We couldn't go back for the dog," Carroll said. "I just remember him running up and down on the island, barking across at us in the darkness."

After a miserable night in the tree, first light revealed that the dog was gone and that the river had risen from 12 to 15 feet in a matter of hours.

"We looked down, and our tree that had been 20 feet above the water the night before was only six feet above the water," Carroll said. "The river was totally whitewater, with trees washing down it."

"When daylight came up we knew we were in trouble," Ferenzak added. "Up until then, we were still discussing whether it was makeable to get to Olowalu. But when we saw the river, we started making another plan."

"Our plan was, 'Let's get out of here — this trip is over,'" Carroll laughed.

Abandoning their hammocks and tarps on the island, the drenched hikers started back down the furious waterway that hours earlier had been a gently purling stream. The rain, meanwhile, began falling even more heavily, cancelling any idea of staying where they were.

It soon became clear that their only hope lay in struggling along one side of the steep bank until they could go no further, then fording the river to the other side, struggling along it, then crossing back before the next cliff. Field-testing this method proved dicier than thinking it up. On the first of their estimated 16 "crossings,"

Ferenzak nearly bought the farm.

He had tied the rope around his waist and started across the river, boulder-hopping where he could. Carroll remained on the bank, paying out the line that lay in a coil at his feet. Neither thought to secure the free end to a tree.

What happened next was that Ferenzak lost his footing and fell into the torrent, which promptly sucked him around a bend and out of sight.

"I stepped off a boulder and I was gone," he said. "All I could see was green water everywhere."

"His weight and the force of the river just ripped the rope right out of my hand," said Carroll. "I got this sudden flash of being very alone."

Fortunately, Carroll had the presence of mind to dive onto the coil of rope at his feet before it was all gone, then roll around a guava tree to brake Ferenzak's wild ride.

"My Christmas present Sunday morning was when he caught the rope and I lived," Ferenzak said, adding that he was finally able to fight his way back to the riverbank and rejoin his companion.

For the next 12 hours, the pair inched down the ravine in the pouring rain, crossing the still-rising river a dozen more times.

"Every time we had to cross, it was a major engineering feat," Carroll said. "Some crossings took an hour and a half, and a few times we had to drop trees across the boulders to get footings."

"There were no more shallow areas," Ferenzak added. "If it was more than waist deep, we had absolutely no chance of making it across."

As Christmas Day waned, the hikers said, they reached a place where they had to do an eight-foot "standing broad jump" from a partially submerged boulder across a raging, 15-foot-high waterfall onto another boulder.

"The river was roaring so loud we had to communicate with hand signs," said Carroll, who went first carrying the rope. "By that time we were starting to get desperate. There was definite frustration. We were exhausted, shivering and shaking. I think we were going on adrenalin alone by then."

Carroll, who weighs about 150 pounds, made the jump with inches to spare, but by the time the 185-pound Ferenzak reached the takeoff spot, it was under water and getting deeper by the second. His partner, meanwhile, was trying to knot the rope around a tree.

"He screamed at me to hurry up, and I screamed back at him to stop screaming," Carroll said. "Then we both realized we weren't going to get anywhere that way, so we both shut up."

Ferenzak finally made his leap, barely catching onto the far boulder with his hands. "There's a boulder up there with my fingerprints in it, like a bowling ball," he joked.

Their packs weren't so lucky. Both went "over the falls" as the hikers strained to haul them across the rapids. Carroll's survived, but Ferenzak's was so demolished by the time they managed to drag it ashore that they simply abandoned it.

By dusk Christmas Day, the two realized they weren't going to get any further, so they clawed their way up the steep bank and dug a four-foot square clearing in the mud. Ferenzak wove ti leaf stalks to form a crude A-frame, then plaited leaves through the framework to make a shelter he hoped would help preserve their body heat through the long Christmas night. They had one sleeping bag left, and it was soaked through.

"We climbed into the bag before dark and stuck our feet into a plastic bag to try and get some warmth," Carroll said.

"We're lying there in the rain and mud in a soaking wet sleeping bag," Ferenzak added, "and he says: 'Oh, by the way, Merry Christmas.'"

It beat spending the night in the guava tree, but not by much. By morning, both men were exhausted, discouraged, frightened, filthy, hungry, drenched and very cold.

Ferenzak's first look around Monday morning brought hope, however, as he saw that the river had dropped two or three feet during the night. They set out at once, fearful that the storm would intensify again. Four hair-raising "crossings" later, at about 7:30 a.m., Carroll reached the major fork in the river that the two had hiked past so light-heartedly 30 hours earlier.

Once they got there, the nightmare was over, for one final crossing would take them to the beginning of a trail, and the trail would take them out of the park.

"I just started screaming for joy," Carroll said.

"I have never felt better in my life than when we hit that fork," Ferenzak added.

A couple of hours later, after stumbling over logs and falling in the mud, the bone-weary hikers finally reached the deserted Iao Needle parking lot, then continued walking down the road until they reached their house.

There they both took the longest, hottest showers of their lives, called the people who would be worried if they didn't show up, switched on the TV set and watched the Rams beat Dallas.

— December, 1983

The Russians

Last Tuesday I went down to Wailea to check out the Russians. I wish I could say it was goodwill that motivated me, or the spirit of world peace . . . but it wasn't. I was just curious.

Mainly, I wanted to see if the Russians look anything like us.

Like a lot of Americans, I had never seen Russians before, but that didn't stop me from forming a clear mental image of them. I pictured them having long, fierce noses and large Adam's apples. Their hair would be dark and very high, their bodies blocky, their skin deathly pale, since there is no sunlight in Russia.

My friend Warren, who has seen Russians up close, told me they also have three elbows . . . but I decided to hold fire on that one. Warren will pull your leg sometimes.

It was a typical Maui summer day: hot and dry, with anything lighter than a Volkswagen bus tumbling toward Kahoolawe in the 40-knot wind. After watching farm animals and tree stumps cartwheel past *The Maui News*, I decided to leave my own bus lashed to its parking place.

I called my friend Naomsky, an American with Russian ancestors and a Japanese car. "You want to go see the Russians?" I asked. "They're down at Wailea painting with Piero."

"Da," she said. "I'll load up the anvils and see you in 20 minutes."

Soon we were rolling toward Wailea, Naomsky's blue sedan secured to the road by a trunkful of anvils. "Do you think they'll look anything like us?" I asked.

"Of course they will," she laughed. "In fact, they'll probably look like me — I'm 100 percent Russian on both sides. My grandparents all came from Russia." I shot a quick glance at her elbows but could only count two.

"But you're 100 percent American now," I said. "You probably don't look Russian anymore."

Ignoring this logic, she wheeled us into the Wailea Shopping Village, where green-and-white striped party tents and a line of blown-down potted palms marked the Russian encampment.

Conditioned by 40 years of Cold War propaganda, I circled the

181

encampment in a half-crouch, my camera in one hand, an anvil gripped menacingly in the other. "Watch yourself!" I warned Naomsky. "They could be anywhere."

Indeed, the place was alive with Russians — I could hear their high-pitched, sing-song language even above the shrieking of the wind, though I couldn't yet pick them out of the crowd. "They're here, all right," I said. "Listen to their weird, sing-song speech."

"That's not speech, you lolo," Naomsky said. "They're singing reggae songs. Why don't you relax and join the party?"

"No!" I said, drawing myself up. "I'm a journalist — it's my job to be skeptical."

"Suit yourself," she said. "I'm going to meet the Russians."

I continued circling in a half-crouch, heart pounding, anvil at the ready. Eventually, led by the unerring instincts of the true journalist, I made my way to the free food tent.

I nearly called Naomsky over to taste the food first, but it looked safe enough — good American staples like tuna sandwiches, diced vegetables, cheese cubes and clam dip. The Maui potato chips had long since blown out to sea.

After triple-loading my plate, I was about to skulk off to some remote corner to feed and ruminate darkly when a young, sandy-haired man of about 16 spoke.

"Would you like something to drink?" he asked. His smile looked American, but his English was slightly accented, and there was a picture of Gorbachev on his T-shirt. Definitely a telltale sign.

"Uh, buh, well, yeah, sure," I stammered, my throat constricting with terror. "I'll have a cocktail! Molotov Cocktail! No! I mean Coketail! Uh, Coke — I'll have a Coke."

He put some ice in a cup and filled it with Coke while I counted both his elbows. "Are you a Russian?" I asked. He nodded pleasantly.

"Are you journalist?" he asked. "I notice your camera. I hope to become journalist. Is hard?"

'Nothing to it," I said. "If you can find the free food tent, you can be a journalist. Pass me that Coke and I'll tell you all about it."

He started to pass me the cup but saw that my hands were full. "Maybe easier if you set anvil down," he said.

It was, too.

—July, 1988

Real McCoy Cowboy

Kawila DeCosta's eyes filled slowly with tears, and his mouth trembled until he could speak no longer.

"You see, he feel sad because he worked hard all his life," his wife Etta explained. "He was the mule of the family."

This man, who in his 82 years has been gored by cattle and dragged by horses, who has slept on frozen ground and lost his old friends one by one; this man who lived in terrible loneliness until he was very old, wept because he had no education.

He was the third son in a family of 20 children, and by the time he was big enough to work, his oldest brother had gotten married, and the second son had run away from home. So Antone "Kawila" DeCosta was taken out of school at the age of 9 to work with his father, John, a woodcutter who raised his family near the forests of Kaupakalua.

Together father and son loaded cords of eucalyptus, koa, rose apple and kukui onto John DeCosta's 14-oxen bullock cart. They drove the cart down the mountain over rutted mud roads to Kailili in the driving rain, stayed the night, and reached the sugar plantations at 2 a.m. the next night.

The wood was needed for the furo baths and cook stoves of the camp laborers, and it was needed all the time. There were no days off. There was no time for school or play or girlfriends. There was only work.

As soon as the wood was delivered, the DeCostas would drive their bullock cart onto the beach at Paia and fill nine barrels with sand. Then they would drive the team past Medeiros Saloon to the Paia railway depot. There they would load a ton each of lumber, cement and gravel onto the cart for the long haul back to Makawao, where the materials would help build St. Joseph's Church.

They didn't make enough money to buy shoes.

"My father always used to go barefooted," Kawila said. "If he put shoes on, he got sick. I went barefooted, too. From 9 until 23, I never wore shoes."

Kawila watched other children go to school, but on the few days when he was allowed to go, they made fun of him because he couldn't read or write. He grew into a strong young man of marrying age, but there would be no wife or children for him.

"My brothers and sisters, everyone got married," he said. "I was the only one stay back."

Finally, in 1923, John DeCosta sold his bullock cart, and Kawila went to work for Grove Ranch near Makawao. He learned to rope and ride and brand, fix fence and cut trail; how to wrap a broken bone with a poultice of Hawaiian salt, koali vine and blue weed.

He became a cowboy. And that is the life he has led for 60 years — at Grove Ranch, at Kaupo, on Kahoolawe and at his own leased ranchlands in Keanae, Nahiku, Huelo and Makawao.

Along the way, Kawila also worked as a mason and carpenter, salted beef and dressed out 800-pound hogs, competed in the first Makawao Rodeo and two others, shot goats for the federal government in the crater, planted pineapple, drove bulldozers and built his own house.

His stories could fill a book. On Kahoolawe, his foreman was Manuel Pedro, who won a wife for $50 in a poker game in Wailuku. His bunkhouse partner and only companion for years was the Hawaiian cowboy Jack Aina, who became a champion left-hand roper when he lost the use of his right arm in a hunting accident.

Kawila speaks with fondness of ranch owner Harry Baldwin, who paid him $40 a month ("big money, those days"), bought him clothes and Fatima cigarettes from Kihei, and let him shoot pheasant one week each year in the Baldwins' own hunting grounds on Maui.

There are tales of catching monster moray eels on Kahoolawe at night with a baited crowbar, killing them by hitting them on the tail, then drying their skeletons into bone necklaces that stretched a full 10 feet when nailed to the bunkhouse wall.

That was one of the few pleasures for Kahoolawe ranch hands. Another was brewing "swipe" from sugar and hops and listening to Jack Aina's handcrank phonograph. A third was pounding on the "musical stones" at Omaulu Hill. And once Kawila saw the "akualele," the flying ball of poison fire from Hawaiian legend.

He and Aina and a few others on Kahoolawe rode herd on as many as 3,000 head of cattle and 700 brood mares, built cisterns and hauled water, swam the cattle seven at a time from shore out to the Kahoolawe Maru or the Maizie C and fed those that died to the sharks of Molokini.

World War II brought an end to all that, and Kawila returned to Maui in time to hear about the shelling of Kahului by a Japanese submarine. He went to work in the crater, shooting goats by the hundred and bedding down in the open on bone-cracking crater nights.

"Cold? It was cold like the devil!" he said. "To keep warm, we put dry ferns in barley bags and stuck our feet inside."

After the crater job, Kawila became an independent small rancher and jack of all trades, pasturing his cattle on leased lands in remote parts of East Maui and driving them single file to the slaughterhouse across miles of jungle gulches, clearing trails by hand.

"I had to cut trail. No more roads, you gotta make your own," he said. "I can tell you all the trails on Maui, how to cut short and go from here over there. I used to drive cattle from Nahiku to Honomanu, then up the mountain. The cattle would follow the horse, because they like to lick the sweat off the horse."

Kawila said he usually worked alone on a horse named Radio, but his dogs Spike and Maile were always alongside, doing the work of three men.

"They round up the cattle by themselves, bring in 15 to 20 head. If some get lost, they go off, find 'em, bring 'em in couple hours later."

He smoked cigarettes for 67 years, at first rolling his own Bull Durhams, later smoking three packs a day of Chesterfields. In February of this year he quit smoking, and now his "breathing vessels" feel better. "I quit," he said proudly. "You make your strong mind, can. Now you can smoke by me, no trouble."

Nowadays Kawila DeCosta works two or three days a week at the DeCoite slaughterhouse, running cattle onto the killing floor because he knows all the ranches' brands.

"I know where to put 'em and which is which," he said. "Oskie Rice cattle get circle W brand. Ulupalakua is slip ear. Nobriga's cattle ears split in the middle. You cannot mix up the cattle, because get hard time."

In his spare time he collects aluminum cans, harvests wild lilikoi, and tinkers with his fleet of aging cars, trucks and jeeps. Oh, and he teases with his bride of four years, the former Etta Lee, now a young girl of 70.

"I married him when he was 78 years old," she said, ruffling his silver hair from behind. "I was a widow, and I knew him because he used to come and teach my kids to rope and ride. He was a lonely man, and I was lonely, so we got married.

"This is the oldest cowboy left," she said, laughing. "The authentic kind cowboy where you sleep in the mountains. This is the real McCoy cowboy."

I asked Kawila if, in all his years in the open, sleeping in the mountains and rangelands of Hawaii, he had ever seen anything . . . well, anything that regular people who sleep in houses don't see.

"I saw a menehune on Molokai," he said. "In 1937 was. Some

kids came running where I was staying. Their clothes was all torn up and dirty. They said a menehune whip them and steal their lunches for school.

"I saw him and chase him with a '29 Chevy truck, but I couldn't catch him. He was like a monkey, the face round, full whiskers. That little legs could move, I tell you.

"I chase him in the truck. I knew if I catch him, millionaire! But he went into the pule fern and hid, and when I got there, he was gone. Magic."

He poured himself a cup of coffee, heaped in two full spoons of sugar and stirred thoughtfully. "I like see him appear to me on Maui," he continued. "If I'm on my horse, I'll rope him. I would get that man, put him in a cage, feed him good and take him around the state. Millionaire, I tell you."

I asked Kawila if he had anything he wanted to tell the people who might read this article.

"The world is beautiful," he said. "Sunshine, storm, cloudy the whole day, the hot sun. People crazy sometimes, but the world is beautiful. That girl now (astronaut Sally Ride), she went to Mars and come back, ain't she happy what the world done for her? She praise up herself and all the people behind her. She would never think she would see something like that."

This man who can do anything, yet cries because he never learned to read and write; this man who has seen both ox carts and astronauts in his life; this man who was treated so roughly by the world, yet who loves it so deeply . . . Saturday morning he will ride as grand marshall at the very front of the Makawao Rodeo Parade.

Cheer for him when he passes by, because he is a beautiful man — a strong, gentle, real McCoy cowboy.

— July, 1983

Antone "Kawila" DeCosta, Makawao. Published July 1, 1983.

GLOSSARY

Below is a glossary of terms used (and misused) in *Shave Ice*. Nothing here is engraved in stone — these are only my "slack key" renderings of island terms popular during the past 40 years. For more accurate definitions of Hawaiian words, please refer to the *Pukui-Elbert Hawaiian-English Dictionary*. Mahalo.

aku — swift, blue and silver, torpedo-shaped tuna known on the Mainland as bonito or skipjack.

Alexander Collection — fashionable interior design and furniture showplace in Wailuku in the mid-1980s.

Alii Room — a section of the Ka Lima O Maui thrift store where a few oddly made clothes hang in lonely exile. A fashion Siberia.

allons! — French for "let's go!"

Artful Dodger — a coffee house and used book store in Kahului.

" 'as why hard" (that's why hard) — pidgin English expression used as a verbal shrug, or to indicate exasperation with some vexing, stupid situation. Its English relatives might be "that's the way it is" or "give me a break!"

au courant — snobby way of saying "in fashion" or up with the times.

baby luau — traditional island party marking a child's first birthday. A big family occasion, with envelopes of money often left for the baby and parents. See also Hale Nanea.

bacalayos — dried codfish.

bagoong — Filipino favorite, a pungent dark relish made from fermented fish blood and entrails, chili pepper water and other powerful ingredients. Regular consumption of bagoong is said to guarantee potency and long life. Not for the faint-hearted.

Big G's — used furniture store in Kahului where journalists and other poor people shop for furniture. Polar opposite of The Alexander Collection.

Bird — Boston Celtic basketball star Larry Bird, arguably the best white man ever to play the game.

bok choy — dark turnip greens (similar in some ways to collard greens) used in stir-fry cooking.

Borgias — ruthless, powerful Florentine family for whom Leonardo Da Vinci designed engines of warfare and amphibious assaults in the early 1500s.

bummahs — pidgin version of "bummer," used by island youths in the mid-1970s to indicate disenchantment. As in "school only bummahs, man."

Burns, John — the state of Hawaii's second elected governor, the late John Burns was one of the architects of the "Democrat Revolution of 1954" that transferred isle political power from the plantation owners to the labor unions. A still-venerated figure.

calabash cousin — island slang for someone who is part of one's extended family but not an immediate blood relative. The calabash (serving bowl) reference may indicate anyone who shared a family's meals.

canec — fiberboard product made of pressed sugar cane waste, popular during the pre-World War II years for ceiling and wall paneling. Rats love it.

cerizos — Spanish-style sausages.

"Cette elegance nuage, ce n'est pas la meme chose" — The author's bogus high fashion phrase; Alii Room French for "this cloud-like elegance, it is not the same thing." Same as what? I don't know.

chako sticks — portable weapon popularized by martial arts movies: two heavy, hardwood sticks attached by a length of chain. Can inflict grievous personal injury.

chop suey — popular stir-fry dish, means "mingled" when used as an adjective, as "her family all chop suey."

chow fun — egg noodles steamed with meat bits and vegetable broth, often served in conical cups at carnivals, fairs and concerts. Very popular.

Churchills — the original body-surfing fins, distinguished from lesser, pretender brands by their fish-tail shape. The classic ones are green and floppy.

chylook — "try look," pidgin for "look at that."

contract bride — as most of the plantation laborers brought to Hawaii were single men, many saved their money and sent back to the old country for a bride. Similar to the "mail order bride" of the American wild west. The ultimate blind date.

crack house — place where crystallized cocaine ("crack") is sold for smoking or injection. Not a good place for vice-presidents.

Crafts — Crafts' Drug, for many years the Maui version of Rexall, complete with an astounding toy and knick - knack department.

Cyrano — Cyrano de Bergerac, a long-nosed romantic hero from French literature who planned to fly to the moon powered by geese.

Earl — Earl "Gabby" Tanaka, long-time *Maui News* editor and softball star and, to his frequent regret, my former boss. Generous, hard-working and considerate; a pillar of *The Maui News* for 40 years.

fivers — military communications slang for the best possible signal reception (on a scale from one to five).

furo — Japanese ancestor of the hot tub; a wood-fired bath that was a popular gathering place in plantation days.

Gorbachev — Soviet president Mikhail Gorbachev, the only world leader ever to upstage Ronald Reagan.

green flash — atmospheric effect often reported when an ocean sunset is viewed on a cloudless evening. The hot green pinpoint visible just after the sun disappears is said to be caused by its last rays bending through the ocean. All of this is subject to endless debate.

Haig — General Alexander Haig, one-time presidential candidate, Nixon advisor and former secretary of state. A powerful name in any appointment calendar.

Hale Nanea — ("house of relaxation") a big, rambling, weather-beaten old oceanfront structure near Kahului Harbor; the site of countless baby luaus and raucous island parties.

hana buttah — there is no polite way to define this. Pidgin for the stuff produced by toddlers' runny noses. "Hana buttah days" usually means early childhood.

hapa haole — haole (literally, "without breath") originally referred to anyone not part of the living breath of the Hawaiian culture, that is, any foreigner. It has since evolved to mean any white person. Hapa ("half") usually refers to an islander with one Caucasian parent. Hapa haole can mean anything where white and Hawaiian cultures mix, as the "hapa haole" music popular in the 1940s and 1950s.

hibachi — portable, charcoal-fired grill popular for isle outings or garage parties.

Hilo Creme — sweet, bland, white flour cookie sometimes dipped in cocoa or milk until the bottom half falls off.

holo holo — to go someplace, whether with a destination in mind or just for pleasure. When cars reached Hawaii, the expression became "holo kaa."

Idini's — popular 1980s lunch spot in the Kaahumanu Shopping Center featuring pasta, salads, white wine and other yuppie foods. An okazu-ya for haoles.

ini quatro — plantation-era marble game.

iwa bird — man-of-war or frigate bird; a large black sea bird that attacks other sea birds and takes their catch. Revered in Hawaii as a consumate flier, the iwa bird also is a harbinger of stormy weather. Sometimes called "storm birds."

jun ken po — rhythmic children's choosing game which uses finger gestures to indicate paper, scissors and stone. One common version is "jun ken-a po, I can-a show, Wailuku, Wailuku, bum bum jo."

kanji — pictographic characters of the Chinese (and hence Japanese) language. There are about 10,000 kanji.

Kapalua Bar and Grill — where the elite meet; an Idini's for trendy millionaires.

kau kau — pidgin Hawaiian from the Chinese "chow chow;" generally refering to a meal or to eating.

keiki — child.

kolohe — rascal, or rascally behavior.

Kona weather — southwesterly winds common during December, January and February may bring still, gray, humid weather and torrents of rain. A winter reversal of Hawaii's usual northeasterly "trade" winds.

lauhala — woven products made from plaited hala (pandanus) leaves soaked in salt water and stripped of their thorns. A durable and flexible matting once used for sails, now popular for hats and floor coverings.

laulau — A savory luau staple featuring pork, beef, salted fish or taro tops wrapped in ti leaves or banana leaves and baked in a ground oven (imu), or steamed or broiled.

Liberty House — where the near-elite shop for clothes, shoes, cosmetics and costly household gimcracks. Maui's Macy's.

lilikoi — passion fruit, a tart mouthful of sweet-sour seeds in a tough yellow skin. Grows on a vine that, left to its own devices, can take over the world.

limu — seaweed generally, but also many kinds of edible seaweed.

linguesa — Portuguese blood sausage, a popular isle picnic staple.

Little Beach — a section of the Makena shoreline separated from "Big Beach" (Oneloa) by a challenging lava ridge; thus, a popular nude sunbathing spot.

lolo — Literally, brains, but popularly used to describe one whose brains may be weak. Also, behavior bordering on the irrational.

lomi lomi — popular name for the Hawaiian massage form of rubbing, squeezing and rolling the flesh to soften it.

luau foot — comical island slang for the wide, flat, tough foot produced by a barefoot lifestyle. Its even wider brother is the "taro patch" foot.

luna — boss, overseer or foreman.

malasadas — Portuguese-style doughnuts made by deep-frying sweet yellow batter in oil. In the modern version, the crunchy crust often is dusted with white sugar. The plural reference here indicates that it's hard to eat just one.

mai-tai — sweet, syrupy rum-and-fruit juice drink popular with tourists. Often served with a pineapple wedge and a tiny paper parasol. Two or three of these can be two or three too many.

manapua — soft, white, heavy, doughy confection with bits of cooked meat inside.

mauka — toward the mountains (opposite of makai, toward the sea). Hawaii's mauka - makai direction system baffles visitors accustomed to north, east, south and whatever that other one is.

MCC — Maui Community College, located between Wailuku and Kahului.

menehune — in Hawaiian lore, a mythical race of small people thought to have inhabited Hawaii before the Polynesians.

MEO — Maui Economic Opportunity, Inc., a federally funded agency with programs for senior citizens and economically disadvantaged families. Its Kahului headquarters is a long manapua throw from MCC.

milk covers — children's game from the days when milk came in bottles capped with flat cardboard discs. The "milk cover" discs would be stacked in a pile, onto which would be hurled a taped milk cover or "kini" heavier than the others. The hurler won any milk covers which toppled off the stack.

mochi — traditional Japanese New Year confection made from rice pounded on a flat surface by heavy wooden mallets.

mushrooms — in modern parlance, any species of smallish, gray, mood-altering mushrooms with conical caps, often found growing from cow manure in isle pastures after a rain. Mildly psychedelic. Also called "shrooms" by grinning devotees.

nah nah nah — pidgin expression meaning "just joking," often quickly appended to a risky remark.

nalu — literally, wave or surf, but also used to refer to the maker of same. Old-time bodysurfers would "call Nalu" for waves by pounding the water with their hands to produce a drum-like boom.

No-Doz — over-the-counter sleep-prevention pills popular for all-night "crash" studying or cross-country driving when I was younger and stupider.

no ka oi — "the best," adopted as Maui's motto.

no talk sweef — pidgin rebuke for one using big words or fancy-kine language.

okazu-ya — cafeteria-style restaurant offering sit down or take-out service of favorite Japanese meals. Very popular for a half-hour lunch.

opu — stomach.

paiute — card game of unknown origin popular with isle old-timers. Did it come from the Paiute Indians?

paipo board — Hawaiian ancestor of the boogie board. In my day, usually a flat, slim, fiberglassed wooden "belly board" with bevelled edges and no skeg. In knowledgeable hands, the fastest of all wave-riding boards, especially on big days.

pakalolo — slang Hawaiian for marijuana, the smoke (paka) that makes one crazy (lolo).

pali — any cliff, but on Maui specifically the ocean cliffs and road segment between Maalaea and Ukumehame.

paniolo — Hawaiian cowboy, from "espaniol." The first cowboys in Hawaii were Spanish.

papio — immature form of the ulua, or jack (crevalle) tuna. Very tasty eating; easier seen than caught.

pau hana — the work is done, or, the end of the working day. There is often an implied "happy hour" feeling to the term.

Peruvian flake — a type of nearly pure cocaine esteemed by drug abusers. One of the higher forms of entropy.

Piero — Piero Resta, energetic Italian artist, actor, restaurateur and impressario. East Maui's most dedicated proponent of creative fellowship, often prevailing against great odds.

pipi — beef.

plate lunch — generic island take-out meal served on a cardboard plate and carried away in a white or pink cardboard box. Must include rice and macaroni salad, along with entree.

poho — tough luck.

poppers — youthful devotees of a dance form popular in the early 1980s. I can't remember the dance — was it like "breaking?"

punee — in modern parlance, any couch or day bed, but old-timers refer to a "moveable couch" made by piling lauhala mats.

pupu — appetizer, anything from boiled peanuts to fancy hors d'oeuvres. "Heavy pupu" usually means grilled meat, sausages, fish, forget dinner.

Puu Kukui — literally "hill of candlenut trees," Hawaiian name for the West Maui volcano whose steep valleys are lush with kukui trees, the oily nuts of which were strung and lit for illumination by the early Hawaiians. The chewed pulp of the nuts was spat upon the ocean to provide clarity for inshore spear-fishing. The nut meat also is an ingredient in the popular Hawaiian relish inamona.

Reyn's — leading Hawaii sportswear company that shrewdly redefined isle fashion in the late 1960s by turning the once-gaudy "aloha shirt" inside out. The classic Reyn's cotton shirt, often in subdued pastels and understated prints, remains popular with isle movers and shakers.

Shark Pit — popular surf "reef break" between Puamana and Lahaina, not far from the popular shark breeding grounds off Launiupoko.

slack key — an island style of guitar playing achieved by slackening the strings to an "open" tuning. Also, a slang term for anything casual and easy-going.

tabis — Japanese-style footwear ranging from thin, soft cotton "booties" for household or ceremonial wear to tough, rubber-soled canvas shoes ideal for reef-walking.

talk story — to "shoot the breeze." May include gossip, but usually a good - natured storytelling session rich with pidgin expressions, dramatic delivery and isle humor. An art form in itself.

tar road — in plantation camp parlance, an oil-surfaced or paved road, as opposed to a dirt road.

T.H. — the late, lamented Territory of Hawaii.

TM — Transcendental Meditation. I'll tell you my mantra if you'll tell me yours.

tournahauler — gigantic trailer-truck built specifically to haul tons of burned sugar cane from field to mill. An awesome sight, day or night.

Trans Pac — the biannual Trans-Pacific downwind yacht race from California to Oahu. Alternates now with the "Vic-Maui" Victoria to Lahaina race.

tres — French for very.

tutu — a grandparent, formerly "tutu kane" (grandfather) or "tutu wahine" (grandmother), but now generally meaning grandmother.

Ulumalu Road — potholed, uneven, semi-paved East Maui residential road guaranteed to jar the traveler senseless.

wahine — woman or female.

won bok — mild, long Chinese cabbage with a white heart, often chopped into soups and salads.

Yoko — conceptual artist and recording star Yoko Ono, an occasional Maui visitor.

Youngblood — Ron Youngblood, veteran Maui journalist, motorcyclist, novelist, broadcaster, playwright and pundit.

zydeco — rollicking, Cajun-flavored dance music from Louisiana, often featuring an accordianist. Listed here because I needed a Z. And zat's all, folks.